To Dick & Ruth

Enjoy!

Jay Kemp

CRITTERS...is a compilation of thought-provoking, humorous, and thoroughly entertaining short stories and poems...Jay Kemp has an unswerving eye and a perked ear that enables him to keep his readers hanging on his words...A potpourri of stories that contain animals that speak and have grand senses of humor, these tales are recommended for their vitality, sensitivity, and charming characters.

Editor: Rutledge Books

Printed in the United States of America.

CONTENTS

This, my first book, I dedicate
to my wife Carol.

CRITTERS
From The Third Planet

BY

JAY KEMP

LIFE

Life is a fragile thing
as fragile as
a butterfly wing.

"CLAN OF THE MOCKINGBIRD"

My name is Al Cox and I'm sitting here at the kitchen table, a yellow legal pad before me, my pen poised. I wonder how to write this story in a manner that won't make me sound demented.

At least a hundred mockingbirds have wedged themselves in and around the kitchen window. This quivering mass blocks out the daylight like a feathered curtain. They watch me with their beady little black eyes and black minds. Although it's almost noon I've had to turn on the lights. As I write, the quiet is eerie and frightening and I know they wait for me to make a mistake and 'change' in their presence.

If I should suddenly disappear without a trace, this story will explain what happened. I swear to all the powers above, that this is a true record of my bizarre adventure. At the moment, it doesn't matter to me if you do, or do not believe it. Right now, my need is to stay focused and concentrate on my writing. The concentration keeps me from 'changing' at the wrong moment, but my mind and body grow tired.

What does 'changing' mean, you might ask. Well, I'll tell you, but please don't laugh, not just yet anyhow. Hear me out. Get ready for this. I have the ability to change from a man into a mockingbird. Now you can laugh, but please read all of my story before you make a judgment.

About a month ago, near the first light of morning, a strange noise woke me from a sound sleep. Not quite wide awake, I lay there with my eyes closed. It sounded as if someone were tapping on the window with a carpenters nail or a finger nail. The sound went tap-tap-tap, then paused for a few seconds, just long enough for me to fall back to sleep. The annoying tap-tap-tap began again. I sat up irritated, all thoughts of sleep gone. On the window sill, silhouetted against the morning light, was a mockingbird tapping on the glass with its beak. My thought was; this is a peculiar, nervy, and bold way for a bird to act.

The bird pecked the window again, turned its head sideways, and looked at me with one eye, as if to say, it's time to get up, flake-head.

Now, under normal conditions I have a good sense of humor and this would have been a laughable situation, however, something about the bird's antics made me furious. I waved my arms and shouted, "Damn you, you feathered pest, get away from there!"

The bird hopped sideways a couple of times, still eyeballing me. It squawked, flew to the patio table where it deposited a mottled gray blob, then brazenly strutted around the table top.

My wife, Sue, sat up, still half asleep, and asked, "What are you shouting about? What's wrong?"

Pointing at the bird, I said, "That damn mockingbird out there woke me by tapping on the window.

I would like to wring its scrawny neck!"

The way she looked at me, I couldn't tell if it were a look of disgust or pity, or if she had turned her hearing aid down on me again. So, I shouted at her, "That bird woke me up by tapping on . . .."

She cut me off and said, "Don't shout, I hear you just fine. I'm sure of it now, Al," she continued. "You have slid right over the edge, lost it altogether, and you had better see a shrink, or I'm going to have you committed." With that said, she pulled the covers over her head, went back to sleep, and picked up her snoring right where she left off..

The bird flew to the window sill again and smacked the glass with its beak, as if to make sure it had my attention. It then flew to perch on the back of a patio chair and broke into song with all the latest mockingbird hits.

Although I don't normally get up before Sue, I made the effort. Spending extra time with the morning paper appealed to me. I might even finish it before Sue got her hands on it.

My morning routine seldom varies: a trip to the John, get dressed, put the coffee water on, and take my assortment of vitamins and Worcestershire sause in apple juce. This morning's routine was different; the bird still on my mind, I opened the back door and stepped onto the patio. The bird was still there, singing its brains out, but took off when it saw me looking for a rock.

I called Cleo, our black cat, "Cleo! Come on. Breakfast! Come catch the nasty bird!" Cleo is like a cop, never around when you need her.

As I opened the front door a car drove by. The newspaper sailed out of a window and thunked on the driveway. Before I could pick it up a mockingbird landed on it, looked straight at me, dumped on it, turned around, flipped up its tail and mooned me. It let out a couple of squawks, that sounded like a horse laugh, then took off for the nearest tree.

It could have been a coincidence or a politically correct statement, but the bird had crapped on the headline about the baseball strike. I grabbed a dollar-sized rock, fit it firmly between my thumb and fingers, and threw it at the feathered pest but missed. The rock sailed on and bounced off the top of my neighbor's car as he backed out of his driveway. He slammed on his brakes halfway into the street and jumped out of his car.

"Cox!" he yelled. "Are you nuts? What the hell are you doing?"

"I'm sorry!" I yelled back. "I was trying to hit that bird. It just dumped on my paper!"

"You are nuts. I suggest you get help. As to your paper, shove it where the sun don't shine!" Back in his car, he slammed the door and flipped me a featherless bird as he roared away.

Forgetting about the pesky bird was impossible. It did the same thing to the paper three days in a row. I don't dare mention to Sue what the bird is doing to the paper. She still looks at me like I'm wacky and threatens to call in the funny-farm wagon.

Today, three mockingbirds are playing games with me, and I can't figure out how to get rid of them, I'm also wondering why they chose me to pick on. Could it be revenge? A few days ago, I caught two of them in the grape arbor and sprayed them with water.

They flew off soaked and scolding. That's the only reason I can think of that would cause them to act this way.

Yesterday, the morning paper looked like it came

from the bottom of a bird cage, only worse. Working as a team, those damn birds have managed to pull the rubber band off the paper and open it up. This gives them a bigger target, more paper to cover. It's true! I watched them do it.

I wear rubber gloves when I peel off the front page, and making up stories for Sue has become a real challenge.

"Where's the front page Al?"

"It got wet. I tore it off. You couldn't read it."

"Has it been raining?"

"Yes, early this morning," I lied.

"It must be raining early every morning. I haven't seen the front page in days. Has something happened in the news that you don't want me to know about?"

I didn't have an answer, so I didn't say anything. She watched me until I couldn't take it any longer. When I left the room, she yelled after me, "You're getting closer and closer to commitment, Al!"

This part of my story is difficult to believe, even for me. It's a real science fiction thing. It happened after a week of mockingbird harassment; I was full up to here with their dirty tricks. I even thought about suggesting to Sue, that she call the medics and tell them to bring a straitjacket. Hell! I was in such a sorry state, I was ready to beg her to call.

What actually brought on the change, I'll never know for certain, but as I remember, it happened like this. Okay! Picture me sitting at the kitchen table.

What's left of the morning paper was spread out in front of me, and I tried to read it, but couldn't, because I was thinking, thinking so intently it consumed every corner of my mind.

My thought was, if I could become a mockingbird, a big mockingbird, I could fly out there and kick some bird-ass. I could beat the crap out of the whole flock, peck their heads and pull out all their feathers. Enjoying my thoughts, I could visualize this scene in my mind. Suddenly I heard a 'pop'. It sounded like speaking the word, 'POP,' and just like that, 'POP', I was a mockingbird perched on the back of the chair I had been sitting in. I continued to read the paper.

The 'change' didn't register with my brain right away. I thought, "*Al, you have a great imagination,*" The trouble was, I felt like a bird and could see my feet gripping the top of the chair. Seconds after the 'change', Sue walked in to join me for coffee. She froze when she saw this bird, me, sitting on the back of the chair. Her mouth open, and bug eyed, she looked at me in disbelief for a second, then shouted my name.

"AL COX!"

When I didn't answer, she started in again, but louder. I'm certain everyone in the neighborhood heard her. To my small ears, her shouts sounded like the roar of a lion.

"AL HUTCH COX!" she shouted again. "GET IN HERE! There's a mockingbird in the kitchen!"

Sue looked huge and frightening to me. Making all kinds of bird noises, I tried to talk, tried to tell her, "It's me! It's me!"

Sue flung the back door open so hard it almost ripped off the hinges. Then she grabbed her straw broom, and said, "I don't know how you got in here bird, but you can just get right out." She swung the broom. Lucky thing for me, she missed. Bad luck for me, because I had no bird preflight training; I felt doomed. Fortunately, my natural bird reflexes rescued me. Like a winged missile I escaped through the open doorway and concealed myself among the leaves of the backyard Chinaberry tree.

Sue stood in the doorway looking in my direction. She shook her broom and shouted, "And don't you dare come back!"

Before I could adjust to the new me, two mockingbirds landed on the branch next to me. Being eyeball to eyeball with a bird was a shock. They looked huge, but I was bigger, almost twice as big as they.

To my surprise, I realized the birds were talking to me. They made bird noises, but in my mind I heard words. Their voices sounded like elves' voices.

One bird asked, "What kind of assignment took you into a human house?"

The other bird sounded female, but still elfin. She said, "What you did was brave. You're lucky you are alive and still flying."

Bird one said, "Are you going to tell us what happened to you in the human's house when you come to the clan meeting?"

Bird two said, "The clan meeting will begin in the grapevine behind the house. We will have a grape lunch first and then move to the big eucalyptus tree next door for the meeting. Will you be there?"

"Yes. I'll be there."

"There's the human's cat on the roof of the house. Let's have some fun; pull some cat fur." Bird Two addressed me again. "Will you join us in the morning, and help us drive the male human crazy? We are getting even with him for spraying us with water."

"I would enjoy that."

While the two birds dive-bombed Cleo, I hoped she would get lucky and snag one of them.

Still in mild shock and perched on the limb, I was

not certain this wasn't just a vivid dream. On the other hand, if it wasn't a dream, I thought it prudent to find out if I had retained the ability to return to my human form. I almost did it right then, but caught myself just in time, realizing it might be a good idea if I got out of the tree first.

Sue opened the back door and called out, "Al! Answer me--where the devil has that nut gone?"

She had a confused look on her face. She stopped calling and closed the door in frustration. I dived from the tree, glided across the yard, and landed on the patio deck just outside the door. Concentrating on being 'me', that popping sound happened again, and the 'change' took place. As quickly as I could clack my beak, I was 'me' again. I opened the door and stepped inside. Sue jumped, spun around, let out a scream, and swung her deadly broom, missing my head by inches.

"Damn you Al!" she shouted, "don't sneak up on me like that. You'll give me a heart attack." She cocked her head to one side, like one of the birds I'd been talking to, and gave me a quizzical look. "I was just out there looking for you and couldn't see you anywhere. Where were you?"

I said, "Calm yourself and put the broom away. What did you want?"

"There was a mockingbird, right here in the kitchen, and I wanted you to chase it out, but you were nowhere in sight, so I did it myself. I still can't figure out how it got in here. Birds don't open doors or windows." Sue paused long enough to take a breath, then started in again, asking where my hiding place was.

I said, "I was not hiding. I was in the backyard behind the shed looking for Cleo. You just couldn't see me, that's all. The bird must have flown in when the door was open."

Sue said, "Al, that's a lie and you know it. What is this bird to you anyhow; a pet? That's it. Isn't it!" She shouted. "I'll bet you let it in on purpose! Is this the same bird you claim knocked on the bedroom window?"

She was really working up a case against me. I cut her off to break her rhythm. "You're getting hysterical, and, no, the bird is not a pet. Besides, it didn't knock, it tapped on the window with its beak, and I don't know if it was the same bird. They all look alike to me."

Convincing her to calm down was not easy. I poured our coffee. We sat at the table reading the paper, minus the front page of course. The birds hadn't given up their dive-bombing as yet.

Reading wasn't exactly what I doing. The words passed before my eyes, but didn't register. My mind was in turmoil. I thought, 'Who in the world would believe such a bizarre story? I can just imagine what they would say; 'Yah, sure Al. It sounds great. You can change into bird and carry on a conversation with other birds? See you around, Al. I'll send you some bird seed.'

Damn it! I know I didn't dream this experience. It was too real! Sue interrupted my thoughts. Her voice seemed to come from a distance. She was repeating my name and saying some unpleasant things.

"Al! Al!" She said as she shook my arm. "I'm sure that article must be wonderful and requires all the attention you can muster with that feeble mind of yours, but pay attention to me for a minute, if you can. Are you listening, Al? This is my bridge day with the girls. You'll have the whole day to yourself to play with that nasty pet bird of yours."

I said, "Thanks a lot. We plan to go flying together. Are you sure you won't join us? *You old bat.*" I didn't have the guts to say that out loud, but I sure wanted to.

She smiled and said, "Al. You really do need some special help. Why don't you turn yourself in and save me the trouble."

When she finally drove off to her bridge club, I took my cup of coffee out to the patio table. My nerves were on edge just thinking about attempting the 'change'. The cup shook and rattled against the saucer as I put it on the table. My thoughts were about finding out for certain, not only if this bird thing were true, but if I could make the change at will.

Placing my hands flat on the table, I concentrated on being a mockingbird, the pop noise came as expected. Presto! as if by magic, I was a bird again. I hopped around my coffee cup a couple of times, then took flight. This was, without a doubt, the wildest day of my life. All the things mockingbirds do seemed to come natural to me; like making strange noises, flying from one tree to another, then up to the top of a power pole to try out some new songs. I sounded darn good for an amateur.

I dived from the pole and glided to a landing on the phone lines leading to my house. I must say here, real or imagined, to fly as a bird was my highest high, ever. The excitement. The feeling of swift, effortless flight was the most fantastic experience I had ever had.

The more I flew the more daring I became, like flying high and circling on rising air currents, then folding my wings and plummeting in free fall, and feeling air rush past me at gale force; then spreading my wings at the last moment and feeling the air slam against them. The force shot me toward the clouds to dive again. What a wonderful, wonderful freedom. I don't know if other mockingbirds enjoy flying like that. If they don't, they're missing out.

Who would have thought a bird could grow tired of flying. Well this old bird was pooped and landed in the Chinaberry tree to rest. Sitting there, I wondered how long my ability to transform myself into a bird would last. Since I had no idea, I decided to enjoy it as long as possible.

Sounds of chattering birds drifted down to me from the top of a tall palm tree. It sounded like several birds squabbling over something, but when I flew up there to find out what was going on, I saw only three birds. They stood in the middle of a palm frond facing each other, but before my feet touched down, they surrounded me. They seemed irritated about something and began asking questions.

The most agitated one sounded like E.T. He asked, "What clan do you belong to?"

Thinking fast, I said, "I belong to one of the local clans. Why?"

"What is your assignment?"

"My assignment?" Having no idea what he was talking about, I took a wild guess and said, "I'm assigned to the house below."

Then he wanted to know if my assignment was the people or the cat. I said, "The people."

The E.T. bird said, "Good thing for you you're not after the cat. That's our job, and we don't want trouble from a single, like you." I never even saw it coming, but the feathered little trickster pecked me hard on the neck; then he continued. "You cause any trouble with us and we will fight!"

The third bird in the group spoke up for me. "You cat-chasers stop making threats!" he shouted. "I am the elder here, and you are breaking clan laws with your threats. Stop it, or your feathers will be before the Chief Council by sundown!"

I had no idea what a Chief Council was, but thanked my new friend and hopped over next to him. He said, "Follow me. We'll fly to another place where those cat-chasers won't bother us."

With rapid wing beats, we flew to the top of a nearby Eucalyptus tree. After we landed, the first thing the elder asked me was my age.

He said, "You appear old and wise, like me. How old are you?"

I told the elder I would be fifty-seven in two months.

He damn near exploded, "Fifty seven!" he shouted. "That would make you the oldest mockingbird that ever lived! Where have you been that we've never heard of you. You must have clan memories we've never heard. I am considered old and wise in clan ways. Only parrots and humans live longer."

Being clever, I said, "I have survived a long time because I have learned to think like a human."

He said, "You must tell all you have learned about humans to a clan elder, like me, and I will tell other elders."

He went on and on about his clan history, beginning from the day he was hatched. The more he talked about clan history, the more boring he became. My only interest was to fly. I thought to myself: what will the clan do if they find out I'm not a real mockingbird, at least I thought I was thinking to myself, because suddenly, a shout from the Elder inside my head shattered my thoughts. "WHAT! DO! YOU! MEAN! YOU'RE NOT A MOCKINGBIRD. IF you're not a bird then what are you?"

With wings stiff and his feathers fluffed out, he was ready to fight.

I said, "I'm a human, but right now, I look like a mockingbird."

Sharing what happened to me with the bird elder seemed like a good idea. If he didn't like it, what could he do about it anyway. Right?

"You're a human? Not a mockingbird?" he shouted, "You're a sick bird is what you are, and sick birds must die!"

With an ear-splitting squawk the elder attacked me with beak and claw, and let me tell you, it hurt like hell. Even though my body was twice as big as his, fighting bird-style was something else. My only defense was to take flight. I plummeted like a rock straight down for fifty-feet before opening my wings, then flew as fast as my wings would beat, heading for my backyard. The old bird elder wasn't far behind, and he was calling in the troops. In seconds every clan member in the vicinity joined in the pursuit, all shouting, "Sick birds must die!"

Making some fancy twists and turns winging through the trees brought me quickly to my tool shed. The door stood open about a foot. Flaring my wings to slow down, I flashed through the opening and landed on a shelf, fully expecting the other birds to follow. Cleo saw me fly into the shed and crouched in the door opening. Her eyes fixed on me, tail twitching, she crept forward preparing to pounce. I heard the elder bird say, "The cat will kill the sick bird."

I sent a powerful thought to the cat . . . "Cleo! Leave--Me--Alone!"

Cleo must have heard my thought because every hair on her body stood on end. She cringed and backed up. I took a chance she would stay distracted for a few seconds, fluttered to the floor, and 'changed' with a pop. My sudden appearance drove Cleo berserk. She tried to scramble out of the shed, but the second her head cleared the doorway, she saw all the birds. Hissing and yowling at this new danger, she did a back-flip into the shed and clawed her way under a pile of rags to hide.

The birds were quiet after Cleo's ruckus. They must have thought she had killed me. When I stuck my head through the door opening to see what was going on, the birds saw me and started their scolding squawks again. Birds were everywhere; on the ground, in the trees, on top of the shed, on the roof of the house, and they were ready to attack.

At that moment, my intent was to reach the safety of the house as quickly as possible. By opening the shed door all the way, I gave myself plenty of room to sprint through it. Pulling an old work hat tightly over my balding head, I dashed toward the kitchen door fifty feet away. I never moved faster in my entire life.

As I cleared the shed door, birds swarmed all over me. They must have decided I really was a man that could change into a mockingbird, and they didn't like it one bit. The birds tried to get at my eyes, but my hands covered my face and I had to peer between my fingers to see. With claw and beak, they tore at my hands until my skin was raw and bloody.

Sue had returned from playing bridge and walked into the kitchen as I ran from the shed. She watched through the kitchen window as this strange spectacle unfolded. Her eyes were wide. Her mouth hung open in astonishment. I heard her shout, "I'm coming Al! Hang on!"

The door flew open. She rushed out swinging her deadly broom and knocked birds in all directions, as if they were badminton shuttlecocks. Sue's broom and shouts scattered the birds just long enough for us to dash into the kitchen and slam the door.

I went to the sink and washed my bloody hands. Sue was looking at me and then at the birds outside the window. She finally found her voice and whispered, "Al, where did all those birds come from?" She paused and looked at the birds again, who were now crowding around the window. "Al, what were you doing in the shed? Al! Answer me! Why were they attacking you? Al! What in the world is going on?"

As I dried my wounded hands, I said, "I'll try to explain, if you will stop talking long enough."

Sue couldn't accept any of my explanation. The more I tried to convince her what happened, the higher she held her deadly broom, which was now in a batting position.

"Listen to me!" I said. "Do you want me to prove what I've been telling you."

She said, "Yes dear," just as sweetly as she could. "I believe you, but if you take one more step toward me, I'll knock your head off."

Exasperated, I said, "Watch this." Then I placed both my hands on the back of a kitchen chair, concentrated, and with a pop! 'changed'. Well, Sue stared at me for a couple of seconds. The deadly broom dropped from her hands. She fainted and slumped to the floor.

The birds saw me 'change' too, and charged the window making a terrible racket trying to get at me. Their voices penetrated the window enough for me to know their plan was to catch me as a bird, rip me to pieces, then scatter my parts to the wind. I tried again to reason with them. To make them understand that their secrets were safe with me, but they still would not listen, so I 'changed' back into 'Me".

Sue recovered from her fainting spell, and I helped her to her feet. She pushed my hands away and backed toward the hall, all the time giving me, The Look.

"Al," she said, "I saw you change into a bird, but still don't believe what I saw. That kind of thing just can't happen. It was a trick, wasn't it Al?"

I said, "No. It wasn't. I did turn into a bird."

"Al, you're insane," she said, "but if by chance you're telling the truth, and I catch you when you're a bird, I'm going to flatten you with the broom, then give your carcass to Cleo to play with, and I hope she eats you. She likes the taste of mockingbirds."

Sue went into the bedroom, locked the door, and called 911. Only her side of the conversation came through the door, but from what I overheard, the cops were going to come after her, not me.

She said, "My name is Sue Cox. Yes! I have a problem. Yes! I think it's an emergency, or I would not have called 911! I will explain the problem if you will just let me! Okay. Thank you. My problem is this. Hundreds of mockingbirds have swarmed in my backyard. They chased Al into the house and he changed into a mockingbird. What? Yes. Al is my crazy husband. I know it's against the law to joke with 911, but I'm not joking; Come see for yourself!" She was shouting again.. "No you can't talk to my husband. He's the one who caused this problem! What did you say? Is this the way you're going to help me? Yes. I heard you," she said in disgust and repeated mockingly, "Call the Humane Society or the Game and Fish Department. Well thank you very much!" Then I heard the receiver slammed down with a vengeance. It was quiet for a minute, then I heard her talking to herself, drawers being opened, then closed. After about five minutes of this, she threw open the bedroom door and marched past me with a bulging suitcase in hand. She didn't look at me or say a word, and I didn't have the energy or the inclination to stop her. I heard the car start and back out of the driveway. I have no idea where she went. That was three days ago.

Most of the birds are still here. They have guard units that rotate. One stays near the kitchen window. Another guards the front of the house. Every so often I make the 'change' and try to reason with them, but they won't listen; they only want me dead. Now, I smile as I write, because this situation has changed in my favor. After today, I may have new adventures to add to this saga. This morning, I succeeded in changing into an Eagle.

SUMMER SNOW

Colors tan, brown, and yellow
Oak leaves fall like summer snow
carried by a gentle breeze
they stiffly drift like snowflakes
to the ground
they rattle their way
across the drive
pile up in drifts
against a wall
Some are caught in a spider web
one spins freely
on a single thread
I think of the rake
down in the shed
and what will it take
to clean this spread
But the winds not through
shaking the trees
I'll rake the leaves later
when there is no breeze.

CRITTER UP A TREE

Through the open window of my writing loft, I heard a strange sound. A sound I had never heard before. I went to the window and listened closely. My first thought was: What kind of bird, or animal would have a call like that? The sound came again, this time, from somewhere in the tree tops; I assumed it was a bird.

My wife was in the yard and she heard the sound too. She asked if I knew what kind of bird made a call like that. I had no idea. To me, the sound was a cross between a Raven and a raucous Mexican Jay Bird. Locating the source of the sound was difficult, because the squawk only came every few minutes. Walking stealthily among the trees, I tried to spot the noise maker, and was rewarded by a repeat call.

From the top of a small oak tree I could see a dark outline of something.

It looked big enough to be an owl, but then the bark came again and the critter changed position.

Moving slowly and directly under the tree, I could see a fuzzy tail hanging down, I thought; 'it's not an owl, but a squirrel with a sore throat,' the squirrel turned its head and looked down at me. Well, Tally! Ho! Toot the horns; Call the hounds, and mount your horses; a fox pup, not much bigger than a tree squirrel, had wedged its small body into a branch crotch near the top. Shivering from fright or a need for its mother, the small wild thing hung on tightly to a small branch.

I never knew a fox could climb a tree. I figured the pup could have easily been treed by a cat, being only half the size of our cat.

I called my wife to come see the strange bird. At first she would not accept the critter was a fox, a raccoon maybe. To me it looked about eighteen inches long from nose to tail.

I called a neighbor, thinking they might enjoy seeing a treed wild young fox. They came and stood by the fence and wondered what they could use to knock it out of the tree, they even suggested shooting the vicious fox pup.

I asked why they wanted to kill it. They said; because foxes kill cats. I pointed out that if anything were killed, the fox would most likely be the one, considering how small the creature was. Their argument was, that young foxes would grow up and become a threat to all cats. They seemed to know all about how a fox kills a cat.

We tried to entice the animal out of the tree by placing a dish of water on the shed roof next to the tree. That didn't work.

The thing now was, what to do about the fox. Was it injured? or stuck in the tree? I called the Payson Zoo to see if they wanted to rescue the critter. They could not because a special permit from the Game and Fish Department was needed to catch wild animals. I next called the Humane Society, they could do nothing, the same story from Payson Animal Control.

When I called the police they gave me the number of the Game and Fish department, in Flagstaff. They answered my call with a recorded message. I left my phone number. They returned my call and I explained the situation to them. Their advice was to leave the animal alone, and when the pup felt safe, it would come down on its own. A couple of hours later the young fox was gone.

HUNGER

There was once
a starving young drummer
who wanted to play in a band
what a bummer
when the band leader
finally asked him to play
he said not today.
My drumsticks are gone
I ett um.

METER

On a table sits
a bowlful of
crispy iambic meters;
Hungry poets sit
round the table.
As they speak,
in meters free,
the bowl begins to empty.
With most good meters gone
or fallen to the bottom,
should the meter bowl,
be filled again
or does the meter matter?

HIDDEN MEANINGS

Mother.
Yes dear.
I want to play grand songs
to move people
with my music.
Yes dear.
I want to stir the soup of life.
To inspire people
to have deep thoughts
when they hear my music.
Yes dear.
Mother.
Where is my trumpet?
On your piano.
I don't have a piano.
Yes dear, I know.

HEARTH CRICKET

In the rolling hills outside Stratford Oklahoma, sits a farm in a most pristine setting. Grassy fields are bordered by isolated trees clumps. Two bountiful fishing ponds wait at opposite ends of the land. The fields surrounding the ponds and the house are home to Meadow Larks, a Quail covey, a soaring Hawk, squawking Crows, and other unseen creatures.

Louis and Nikki had recently retired there and rebuilt the old house that had belonged to Nikki's parents. My wife, Carol, and I were there visiting.

In late summer, the farm and the house had been invaded by crickets. Although Nikki had sprayed and swept, one cricket managed to escape her. Our first night there I heard a single "Chirp", it was loud, and annoying. I asked what made the strange sound.

"Oh!" said Nikki with pride, "That's our Hearth Cricket. It brings us good luck."

For the next two days it interrupted our conversations. Most times, it sounded as if it were in the room with us. Other times the chirp sounded as if it came from the next room, where Nikki's electronic typewriter sat on her desk. Next to the desk are shelves loaded with books.

The chirp gradually faded into background and we ignored it. It didn't seem to bother their two dogs at all. However, on arising one morning we found Nikki in the living room, spray can in hand. She thought she had located the pesky cricket's hiding place.

We watched her stalking the room as she listened intently and waited patiently. She said, "I've had all the good luck from you I can stand cricket! You are going to die." The critter remained silent until the moment Nikki gave up and left the room. "Chirp", it taunted.

The sound wasn't constant. Sometimes it was hours, sometimes minutes between chirps. The more I heard it, the more I thought it sounded electronic than insect. Carol thought it had something to do with the military aircraft that flew in the area, or maybe it was a faulty air filter, or maybe the house had been bugged.

Whatever this invisible critter was, it had four retired adults baffled. Moving my head in an arc, I tried using my ears like echo-locators, but I guess that only worked for bats.

At first, I thought the sound came from the TV. I stationed myself next to the set in rapt attention. The chirp came in a few seconds, not from the TV, but from the next room. Maybe it was hiding among the books, or maybe it was coming from the typewriter. I stood next to the machine and dared it to make a noise. The chirp was loud and near my left ear. "Chirp" it went, just once. I turned my head quickly and there it was, motionless and all white, it sat on the shelf at my eye level. I grabbed it with both hands and took it into the living room.

Nikki was in the kitchen fixing us breakfast. Louis

and Carol were in conversation by the coffee table. I interrupted them by plunking the culprit on the coffee table and announced: "I have captured your Cricket." Louis and Carol looked at it, smiled, then looked at me, Louis said, "Are you serious?" Nikki shouted from the kitchen: "Kill it! Kill it!"

They were all dumbfounded, until it went "CHIRP", right on cue. We all began to laugh as Louis grabbed it, pried it open and pulled out its heart; a run down battery that had been trying to tell them, with a chirp, "The smoke detector needs a new battery."

DAY BY DAY

The day rose swiftly
then departed with great haste.
Tomorrow waits to do the same.
Tomorrow is loaded with burdens
to dump along the way
burdens to mix and mingle
with those left over from yesterday.
Some burden piles grow large
some stay small.
Large or small
they disappear with
the shrug of a shoulder
none more important
than the other.
Good or bad
wanted or not
count on tomorrow
to unload something new.
What am I to do
What *am* I to do

No Need To Hurry Anymore

Since I retired, I've made plans
for all the things I'll do
now I have time to think them through.

There's no need to hurry anymore

The family is gone
I've no deadlines to meet
or decisions to make
I plan to enjoy my solitude
I sit in my chair and watch TV
a bowl of snacks within easy reach
Now the snack bowl sits empty and begging
I tried to remember a thought that I had
but whatever it was has left me. Oh! well

There's no need to hurry, anymore

Time passes swiftly, the phone rarely rings
I fall asleep in my chair quite easily
I awoke late one night
the TV still on and hissing
I sat there and watched
black and white dots
jump all over the screen
I've sunk deep in my chair
and as if we were one the fabric enfolds me
but I really don't mind

There's no need to hurry, anymore.

THE CROSSING

"Mother, why do we have to get up so early?" Complained the young son.

"You know very well why. Now go wake your sister and we will leave this place, and son, be very quiet."

As quietly as he could, he walked to where his sister lay sleeping, put his mouth against her ear and whispered loudly, Sister! Sister! It's time to get up!"

She answered in a sleepy voice, "Why are you waking me? It's still dark."

"Mother will tell you why. Now come on."

Side by side, they walked quickly to where their mother waited.

"I still don't understand why we have to travel in the dark."

The mother, on guard, and alert to any strange noises, waited to answer her son's question.

She said, "I'll explain it to you again. This time, you must listen very carefully to what I tell you and your sister. Come stand close to me. Some day your lives may depend on what I tell you. Are you both listening?"

"Yes mother," they answered together, then moved close to each other for warmth. Still shivering, they looked up at their mother in rapt attention.

"Do you remember when we were here before? We were late getting to the road. Do you remember what happened?" "Yes, I remember that. I was very frightened, and so was sister."

Sister interrupted, "I remember too. Cars were speeding by and we couldn't cross the road. We had to hide all day and cross late that night."

"That's right!" Said Mother proudly. "See, you both remembered. Now. Let me repeat what I told you before. Another reason we must cross early, before the sunrises, is so we won't be seen.

If we are seen, the cars will stop, and the people will chase us, and we will have to hide again!"

"But Mother, why do we have to cross at this place? There are many places we could cross," said sister.

"I'll explain as we walk. This trail is special. It guides us to a meeting place in the woods across the highway. Now listen to me.

When we arrive at the crossing point, stay close to me, and when I run, you run with me--we will all be safe in a little while. Your father is waiting in the woods by the stream, and if we are late, he won't be there."

Mother, and her trembling offspring waited in hiding. They waited, and listened for just the right moment. When mother couldn't hear or see any cars, she said, "Now! Run! Run with me!" she dashed across the road, her young ones at her side. The danger and excitement caused their hearts to pound fiercely. Seconds later, they disappeared silently into the dark forest.

Bird songs intrude on the quiet early morning. Wind passing through leaves creates a restful and pleasant sound, then slowly, the first sunlit rays reach over the mountain to cast long shadows that slid down through forest trees. A single light-ray spotlights the words on a sign at roadside. It read: CAUTION!
                        DEER
                     CROSSING

TIME CURE

Eons old
old mother earth
in spite of her girth
allows her tormentors
to plunder her soil
and her soul
until she rebels
with quakes and shakes
then cleans her face
with salty seas and lakes of mud.
When man's endeavors aggravate
she throws a fit of rage
shaking his technology
into piles of rubble
and buries it all
with time.

FROG'S HAVE NECKS

What makes a frog a frog and a toad a toad? I have no idea. They all look alike to me. The difference between a ground frog and a tree frog, is a tree frog has suction cups on the ends of its toes. That's the extent of my frog knowledge.

Last summer, with a book in hand, I prepared to sit on my shady front porch and read. It's not unusual to find wind blown leaves on the porch and chair seats. On the seat of a white plastic chair, I saw what looked like a fat leaf and assumed it had fallen from a hanging plant next to the chair.

Leaning down to brush the leaf away discovered it was not a leaf but a frog about the size of a silver dollar. Body decorations consisted of a light greenish-gray skin covered with turquoise blue warts. In the center of each wart was a coal black dot.

Looking closer revealed the frog's eyes were closed, and his legs were pulled in close against a his shinny body.

The critter was asleep and unaware of my presence.

I must have disturbed the creature because his eyes slowly opened to slits, then to my surprise, he tilted his head back and looked up into my face. He seemed to say, "What are you looking at? Haven't you ever seen a beautiful frog before?"

Frog's have necks?

I would have studied the princely croaker longer, but our curious cat had to see what had my attention. Upon seeing the frog, she jumped into the chair, and gave him a prod with her paw. Naturally, Mr. Frog took exception to this interruption of his nap and leaped to the smooth vertical back of the chair. He stuck there! He then tilted his head again to keep an eye on the ready to pounce cat.

With my face about two feet away, I could clearly see small round sucker cups protruding from the ends of each toe. By golly, this must be a tree frog!

Those little toe suckers must be mighty powerful. When the cat moved, the Leaper leaped and stuck to the wood siding of the house. Before the cat could move again, the warty prince sailed almost five feet to the edge of the porch, then quickly disappeared as he hopped into the foliage below. For the next hour the cat prowled the bushes looking for the frog.

Frog's have necks?

CUDDLING

On winter nights
when bed sheets are cold
we go to bed early
she on her side, me on mine.
We lie on our backs
and warm our spaces
fall asleep
and the snoring begins.
We move close together
spoon fashion to cuddle.
That loving feeling
is still there
she feels as good to me now
as she always has.
But, as happens
the body heat rises
to interrupt
the pleasure of our cuddle.
We turn on our backs
she snores louder than me
I listen to the rhythm
one snore in
one snore out.
I move to her side
my mouth close to her ear
and with a whisper
I say, turn over dear.

CUDDLING TWO

He sez I snore
louder than he
but how can he know
not awake like me.

He isn't awake
when a snort
a wheeze
no breathing a all
are all noises
next to me.

I close my eyes
with the pillow
I cover my head
I don't poke
the old geezer awake
or roll him over
in bed.

I just accept snoring
as if he sneezed.
How can he say
I snore louder
than he.

By Carol Kemp

About Chipmunks and Cats and Brooms

Normally, I sleep later in the morning than my wife, Carol, and being a light sleeper, I sleep with ear plugs. One morning, I heard an uncommon commotion coming from downstairs. Shouting and thumping noises penetrated my earplugs. I removed them and heard Carol shouting at Cleo, our cat. My first thought was, someone or something had invaded our home, maybe a forest creature, such as a bear, a raccoon, or even a skunk.

I hurried to the kitchen, ready to do battle, to defend our home. I wondered what catastrophe had taken place. Carol shouted instructions to the cat, "Catch it! Catch it!" as she tried to dislodge the beast with a broom by probing behind the cabinet.

Cleo darted from one side of the cabinet to the other, each time she reached a clawed paw into the small space. The critter continually squealing its displeasure. Not being able to see what the cat was after, I said, "Catch what? What's back there?

Carol said, "Cleo caught a chipmunk and brought it in before I could stop her."

It must be instinct that directs a wild creature to hide in a smaller place than its attacker can follow. The chipmunk had chosen the three-quarter inch space behind a china cabinet and the wall as a refuge. My solution to the problem was with a yard stick, with it, I managed to dislodge the animal. The black-flash cat caught it. Two humans, one with a broom the other with a yard stick succeeded in chasing the cat with a chipmunk in its mouth out through the open back door.

Wait! it ain't over yet.

Once on the back porch, I grabbed the cat and forced her to release her prize toy, which was still very much alive. Now, you would think a wild thing would head for open spaces, but Noooo! It dashed back into the house, with me, Carol, *and* the cat in hot pursuit. The place it chose to hide this time was a mistake, it tried to find and opening among the paper grocery bags stuffed tightly between the refrigerator and the kitchen counter.

Yardstick and Broom went into action again, and we chased the critter from its intended hiding place. In a dash for freedom, the chipmunk raced out through the door, sped across the porch, down the steps, across twenty feet of open space, then up a thirty foot pine tree. At one point in the pursuit up the tree, I saw the chipmunk on one side of the trunk, and Cleo on the other, until they both disappeared from view in the thick foliage. The carnivore was just inches away from recapturing its victim.

The brave and determined Chipmunk must have found a good hiding place up there, and escaped the Jaws of Doom. After a while, the Jaws of Doom gave up the chase, and returned to earth.

WINDS WAY

Wind come along, fuss with the trees
Wind come along, jiggle the leaves
those pretty October leaves
Strong winds blow, pretty leaves learn to fly
scatter like painted Butterfly
Naked tree look down
watch its clothes scatter on the ground
Stubborn leaves cling tight
no wish to fall or take flight
Tree feels good to have them there

Wind come along pushun cotton white clouds
change white to rabbit gray
then fills them clouds with winter tears

Wind come along, fuss with the clouds
shake um, make um thunder till sparks fly
Squeeze um hard till tears fall free
knock them stubborn leaves off the tree
Wind come along cold
turn tears snowflake white
blow um around, tree catches some
watches most float down
cover leaves on the ground
Be this way for a long time now
be along time till it see a plow.

OLD SHEP

During her senior year in high school, Lola had a memorable experience; a voice spoke in her mind. The unusual event took place in the shade of the ancient oak tree at the edge of her father's farm.

Every school day ended the same for Lola. After departing the bus, she stepped back from it, slipped her book pack over her shoulder, and waited at the side of the county road. From there she waved good-bye to her friends. When she heard the bus door hiss shut, she closed her eyes tightly, clamped her hands over her face and held her breath. Not until the roar of the bus and the diesel fumes died away, did she breathe again and open her eyes.

Directly across the highway from the bus stop was a sign nailed to a post that read: "Paradise Farm". Next to the sign began a double grooved trail that led to her house, a tiresome half mile trudge up hill.

Her dad called this rutted dirt road his Highway to Paradise, and over the years it seemed to Lola this wondrous place truly was a piece of paradise; she loved it there.

At the top of the rise grew a majestic and ancient Oak tree. The old oak waited a hundred feet or so off the trail. Its welcoming branches spread wide. Its roots anchored deep, and unseen. Her father liked to brag about it, and say: "Why, that tree is so old and so big, it must have been the first tree planted by Him when He made this place."

To Lola, it was more than just a giant tree that provided shade; it was her private sanctuary. It was there in the shade she stopped to rest after the tiring climb. Sitting with her back to the Oak's massive trunk, she could look out over the vast farmlands and fields of Barley surrounding her and the tree. Once, she tried to imagine what it would feel like to be the only living person on the planet, but she could not; especially when she thought of Billy Gregory, the handsome boy in her chemistry class.

Some days Lola did her home work at the tree, but on others, she read from a dog eared romance novel being passed among her girl friends. She kept the book hidden in a hollow place at the base of the tree.

When Old Shep, Lola's dog, felt up to the task, he would wait for her at the tree. After geeeting each other, she would take the book from hiding and get comfortable leaning against the tree. Shep would lay his head in her lap and listen while she read a few pages aloud to him. As always, Shep would drift off to sleep, then later, when Lola finished reading, she would shake him gently awake and they would walk slowly home.

They walked slowly because, like Lola, Shep was almost sixteen. Old age and arthritis in his hips prevented him from coming to the tree as often as he had in past years. On those days, Lola missed his company.

Then one day as she approached her private place, she heard a voice, a strong, deep, voice.

It said, "You're late, Lola."

It sounded like her fathers voice, but she wondered, "Did I hear that voice with my ear, or in my mind? Maybe Dad is hiding on the other side of the tree trying to trick me." But when she looked, there sat Old Shep. His eyes were bright and he was smiling; at least it looked that way to Lola. Of course, a dead give-away to his happiness was the steady swing of his tail.

Lola said, "Hi, Old Shep. Is dad here with you? I thought I heard his voice, but I guess I must have imagined it." She put it out of her mind then sat in her favorite place next to the tree. Shep sat next to her and she stroked his head.

This time the voice startled her. "Don't be frightened, Lola. It's just me, Old Shep, talking in your mind." Lola could not believe she was hearing her dog's voice. If she were to tell any of her friends about this, they would surely think she had flipped.

Then the voice spoke again, but this time it was not such a shock. Shep said, "I just wanted to tell you how much I have loved you since I was a pup, and to tell you that the time is near for me to leave for doggy heaven, as you used to call it. Lola told him not to think of leaving; that he would be with her for years to come. Then Shep said, "Lola. Would you hug me for awhile?"

She held him tight with both arms, as she had done many times before. He grunted and sighed with the pleasure of their closeness. Shep's words had been sharp and clear. Now, it seemed natural to hear him speak in her mind. Lola felt the powerful bond of love between them grow stronger.

Their quiet moment ended when Shep stood, turned suddenly, and scooted off like a young pup. She thought he wanted to play, and laughing, she chased after him as he disappeared around the tree. She could not hear or see where he went. Then just as her confusion deepened, she felt his slobbery mouth close lightly around her ankle, and at the same time she heard his distinctive voice.

"Gotcha again Lola."

She said, "Stop that Shep," and patted his gray head. His tail wagged briskly a few times, then stopped. He looked intently into her face. It was a sad worried look. Then his old eyes brightened and he scampered off into the barley field and out of sight. His drool turned cold through her stocking.

Lola waited for him to return, but when he didn't, she cupped her hands to her mouth and called.

"Shep! Here Shep! Please come back!" His name echoed across the fields, but it was not an echo she heard. It was Shep saying in her mind: "Remember me Lola."

A sudden wind swayed the giant Oak and the essence of Shep's voice blended with the sighing sounds of wind passing through its leaves. Abruptly the wind stilled, and there followed an eerie calm. Lola called his name again, and again, but he was nowhere to be seen. He had vanished.

She thought, "Maybe Shep really knows his final hours are near and he has gone to a secret place to be alone."

Lola's heart was full of love for Old Shep, and she cried for him as she walked down the slope to the house.

Her mother waited on the porch and the first thing she said was, "I'm sorry to tell you this honey," She hesitated, then continued. "Old Shep died early today."

Lola stammered, "But I, I just saw him up there by the oak tree. He sneaked up on me and slobbered my ankle, like he always does." As proof that it happened, she felt her still damp stocking.

Her mother cocked her head to one side and squinted her eyes; the way she did when she thought her daughter was fibbing, then her mother continued, "I don't know what you saw, but it sure wasn't Old Shep. Your father and I buried him up there by the oak tree this morning."

The Retort

I walk a different path
than you my friend.

Do not burden me
with the thrust of
your religious beliefs.

I walk in deep green forests
known only to me.

I walk on secluded paths
known only to me.
I commune with a higher intelligence,
not one mind, but many.

My temple can be found only by me in the hills and
valleys of my mind,
hills that stretch beyond
my mind's horizon
to the farthest reaches
of the unending universe.

LOVE

Lay your beauty next to me
Let me enfold you
Let us relive the magic
of skin closeness
of pressing lips
of passion.
Let our auras mix
until they explode
into
fracturing
shattering
living
breathing colors
as
rainbow rays
through crystal.

The Boy Who Loved Crabs

Wind-driven, white-capped waves batter and shape long sandy beaches, the ends of which cannot be seen.

Bare foot, my seven year old grandson, and I, beach comb the ribbons of refuse tossed out by the sea and left on the beach by the last high tide. We ignor the discarded man-made things.

This old man cherished the sea.

We wander north for a while, then south, selecting prize bits of rubble.

"Look there John," I said, "a red-coral fan half buried in the sand, and there, all those colorful sea-shells."

We saved the best ones.

Footprints ahead show we are not the first to pass this way in search of treasure.

They missed a white sun bleached bird skull and a blue-crab claw as big as a fist. What a pinch it could have given; then a partial skeleton of a sea-bird, and dead trigger-fish. We walked around that.

We passed rows of sea-weed that held onto strange junk, like a frayed two inch hawser with a knot still tight, and a piece of broken deck plank.

Jay Kemp

"Where did the rope and board come from Grampa?"

"Well, John, maybe a terrible storm sunk a ship, way out there in that vast ocean; the Sea of Cortez."

"Do you realy think that happened Grampa?"

"I've heard stories like that."

The distant horizon separates the sky and breaking waves with a rippling band of blue-green water. Tides changed. Pushed in. Slid out, leaving rough coral reefs exposed to the bright sun. Tide pools form creating temporary homes for strange creatures, some never before seen by the John, or this old man.

Hermit Crabs crawl everywhere, their actions comical to watch as they drag their cumbersome shell-homes. Cat's-Eye slugs slam their multicolored trap-doors closed when disturbed.

We watch crabs no bigger than a fingernail disappear with amazing speed, but never as fast as the hands of youth. The small creatures try to defend themselves with minute ineffective claws.

John finds Wiggly-Worms in a coral hole, they look like centipedes, some no bigger than tooth picks. They quickly join the growing zoo in the bottom of a plastic cup.

"Look Grampa," John shouts, "a monster blue-crab nearly two-inches wide."

"Can you catch it boy?" I asked.

"Oh yes!" he cried out with glee, "I love crabs."

With its pinchers held wide and high, the crab waited for his attacker, but swift young hands prevailed again. Reluctant to join the zoo, the giant crab fought valiantly and clamped a mighty claw on the web between two fingers. I told my pal, "Let go of the crab, and it will let go of you."

"But I love this crab," declared the budding marine biologist as he danced from one foot to the other. Grimacing painful ouches through clenched teeth, he stoically held onto the crab, and it held onto him.

Seeing the youngsters pain and determination, and before the monster from the deep could draw blood, I worked my Grampa magic and squeezed the crabs back and belly between grizzled fingers; the mighty crab released its victim and I dropped the critter into a shallow pool.

Hand in hand, we two adventurers retreated from an incoming tide. We walked across wet crunching sand, then up the sloping beach through dry sand so hot it burned the bottoms of our feet.

We found refuge from the heat in the shade of a beach umbrella. Relieved, I sat and brushed the hot sand from my feet. John stared with fascination at the wondrous creatures in the depths of his hand-held aquarium.

"Grampa."

"Yes, John?"

"I don't care if the big one got away, I still love crabs."

SECRET

FORMULA

PROLOGUE

Jack stood in the kitchen looking down the hallway toward his darkroom door. He frowned as his eyes locked on the door opposite, the one to the spare bedroom where he had caught his sweetheart Jill and his best friend Bert in bed. Even the hallway brought back angering, hurtful thoughts. He could still see the trail of clothes that led to the bedroom.

Those feelings coupled with feelings of apprehension and discomfort gripped him. His eyes were blood shot and burning. Tears ran from them as if from open faucets. The handkerchief he held over his face was not thick enough to filter out the rancid odor that filled every room of the house.

Because of the consequences created by this stinking situation, Jack saw his plans for a career in photography begin to dissolve.

Jack Stump dreamed constantly of the day he would escape from his dreary job as a student counselor at

Phoenix College. When not counseling, he spent all of his spare time, energy, and money on Photography.

His photo work had been published in newspapers and many magazines. He had three covers to his credit and two one-man shows in a Scottsdale gallery. Having won several awards and photo competitions, he was considered among the best by his contemporaries.

Although Jack had many reasons to be proud of his work, they would have to wait. He had just come from a very disagreeable confrontation with his neighbors and two Phoenix Police officers in his front yard. Officer Turkel's harsh shouted words still hung in the air.

"Listen to me, Mr. Stump, I hope you understand my words. Either you get rid of this putrid odor yourself, or the city will send a hazardous waste crew to do it for you, and you will pay the cost, plus penalties. If you don't clean it up, I personally, will see that you spend time in a cell! Have I made myself clear?"

Jack had said. "Yes! Yes! I understand."

As disgusting as the odor was, Jack had to smile when he recalled how the beet-red face of police officer Turkel and his partner changed to that of chalk-faced Zombies, and gushing tears streamed down their cheeks. Jack could still picture the comical scene as they ran to their cruiser, piled in, then burned rubber for half a block in their haste to out-distance the offensive nose-wracking odor.

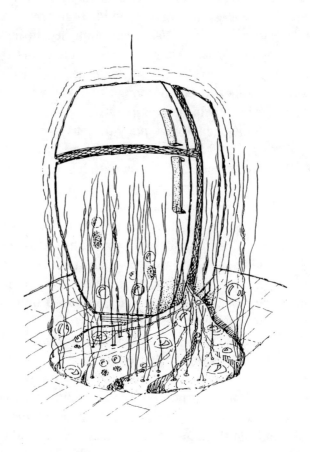

ONE

T-G-I-F. T-G-I-F. Jack Stump used this acronym to keep a rhythm to his Friday jog through the park. In his mind he pictured the letters individually and large, repeating each letter with every foot fall. Normally, this chant helped keep his timing, and kept him from thinking about his boring job; but this morning the chant did not work. Strong disruptive thoughts about how he felt trapped in his job kept entering his mind.

Jack thought, 'Damn, here's that let's-feel-sorry-for-Jack routine again. I know it's a good job, but I'm bored with it. T-G-I-F. I have been a Student Counselor at City College for almost eight years; the job is going nowhere and neither am I. T-G-I-F. I would rather be at home working in my dark-room.

'I feel as if I'm wasting my time at the college. T-G-I-F. At least photography gives me a sense of accomplishment. Although I have a few friends on the faculty, I don't seem to fit in comfortably with most of them, especially Dean Smith, the old grump. T-G-I-F.

'For whatever it's worth, my students do call me

Mr. Stump, and sometimes, on rare occasions, my guidance has actually helped a student and I'm thanked for it. Mostly, I think they laugh at me behind my back--OKAY! OKAY! Enough of the self pity.'

Jack was making good time. He would follow his usual Friday routine when he got back to his old house-- take a long hot shower, dress, have something to eat and walk to work.

As Jack continued his T-G-I-F jog, he thought, 'Shoot. I'm only thirty; so what if I'm skin bald on top; so what if the hair I have left is shot with gray. I have my health; I'm in good shape; Two-ten isn't overweight for a guy almost six feet tall. What the hell--I feel good! T-G-I-F.'

Actually, Jack was five foot eleven and one half inches tall, but when anyone asked his height, he fibbed slightly, stood as tall as he could, and said he was six feet even.

As he jogged along, he listened to the sounds and took in the colors of this pleasant park. It was one of his favorite places. He looked through the trees toward other paths and saw many people running and walking, as well as couples strolling hand in hand. A bike breezed passed him. He watched as its rider turned off the trail and cut across the grassy field to a place in the shade where friends waited.

Farther ahead on the trail, a stunning woman with shoulder length red hair, speed-walked toward him. Her hair and breasts bounced to the rhythm of her walk. She had Jack's full attention. He thought, 'I have seen her in the park before--when we get closer I'll put on my best smile--maybe turn and jog beside her--see if she will stop and talk.'

On an intersecting path, another man jogged at the same speed. He too was directing his full attention toward the speed-walker and abruptly collided with Jack. This sent both men sprawling on their butts.

Without speaking, they exchanged surprised looks and embarrassed grins, then quickly returned their dazed gaze back to the red-head. Their collective unspoken thought was, she looked even more attractive from their ground position than she did at eye level. As she approached them, the swinging beauty put on speed, held her head high, and looked straight ahead. Then, without so much as a glance in their direction, she walked past them, a big smile on her pretty face.

Knowing the two men continued to ogle her, her swing became more seductive and her sway more animated and enticing. Not until she was out of sight did they help each other off the ground.

"What a great performance! I hope she didn't hurt herself with all those body moves." The man laughed and held out his hand. "Hi. I'm Bert Simon."

"Pleased to meet you, I think, considering our brief and abrupt encounter. I'm Jack Stump. Where were you headed?"

"For the parking lot. I've had enough excitement for the day. What about you?"

As the men dusted themselves off, each sized up the other.

"I'm going in the same direction. Why don't we finish our jog together," said Jack.

"Fine with me."

They started to jog at an easy pace, but as they approached the parking lot, their macho Ids kicked in and they tried to best each other. They arrived at the parking lot in a dead heat. Bert stopped suddenly and leaned against a late model station wagon. Jack's momentum took him down the walkway a few feet farther. He stopped and jogged back to join Bert. Bent over, hands on knees, he gasped for air. Bert was in no better condition. It was at least two minutes before either man could speak.

In a winded voice, Jack said, "That's a good looking station wagon."

Bert smiled and said, "Yes it is," then walked to a new Porsche parked next to the wagon, reached through the open window and retrieved a sweat towel. With a towel end in each hand, he flipped the middle over his head and behind his neck. Then with a pridfull voice said, "This, is my wagon."

Jack had a major attack of instant envies. It triggered his over active imagination. He pictured Bert, and his bright red symbol of wealth, in a dream scene. In the first scene, Bert was posing with Red the speed-walker. Her skimpy swim suit would have fit easily into Jack's shirt pocket with room to spare. Her hands and head rested coyly on Bert's shoulder. The scene changed, the way you would flip through a new stack of film prints.

Now it was Bert in a polo outfit. Red wore the same swim suit. Bert in a tennis outfit; Bert in swim trunks; then in a tux. Red was there in each pose, still wearing the same swim suit, only now Jack saw her as a cardboard cutout posing with Bert.

"What are you driving Jack?"

Lost in his dream world, Jack didn't hear Bert and continued to fantasize about the Porsche, only now, he saw himself posing with Red.

"Jack? Where are you?"

Bert's calling summoned Jack back from his dream.

"Oh! Sorry, I was daydreaming about your red wagon. It must be great to drive such a sporty car."

"It's a real dream-boat all right, and impressive with the ladies."

Jack thought, 'I'll bet he gets all the ladies he can handle. Just look at the smug bastard. He makes me sick, standing there posing beside his Porsche. With his full head of hair and his perfect white-toothed smile, he makes me look like a toad.'

"You didn't tell me what you're driving."

Jack was almost ashamed to tell him, but he did.

"It's a custom Ford bucket of loose bolts. It has over a hundred thousand miles on it and needs a new engine. It runs when I need it to." Jack was beginning to feel defensive.

"Do you have any plans to restore it?"

"Maybe, someday, when I have the time and money. I'm fortunate to live within walking distance of work; I only drive the heap on rainy days."

Bert handed him a business card.

"Give me a call before you leave work and let's get together someplace for a drink--your choice."

Jack didn't read the card just then, but stuck it in his sweaty pocket.

"Sounds good to me."

Bert tossed his towel through the open window and climbed into his lady-bait car, closed the door, and stuck his head through the sun roof opening.

"If you have a lady friend, bring her along and we'll make a night of it."

"I just met someone new. She might enjoy a night out. Her name is Jill."

"Jill? As in Jack and Jill? Do you live on a hill?"

Bert laughed as if what he said were the funniest

words ever spoken. "I'll see you later." Jack could hear Bert's laughter trailing behind as Bert drove to the parking lot exit.

"If I ever see him again, I think I'll choke him." He took Bert's business card from his pocket and read it aloud.

"SIMON DRAKE and SIMON, ATTORNEYS AT LAW, BERT SIMON - ASSOCIATE. Well whoop-de-do, Mr. Bert Simon is a big shot lawyer."

Jack stuck the card back in his pocket and jogged toward home.

Just past the entrance to the parking lot was a bus stop. When Bert turned the corner, he saw Red the Speed-walker sitting on a bench at the bus stop. Next to her sat two elderly ladies. Naturally Bert pulled to a stop at the curb opposite the bus stop, popped his head up though the open sun roof, and spoke to Red. She seemed pleased and smiled broadly.

Bert said, "Hi! Remember me? I fell head over heels for you in the park."

She giggled girlishly. "Yes. I remember you, and the other man."

The two older women on the bench next to her, Audry and Mavis, were as different as night and day. Audry sat stiff back straight, both hands holding tight to her purse. She looking straight ahead, mouth puckered and eyes squeezed half closed.

Every line in her face showed disapproval, but she did listen to the exchange. Mavis, however, was all smiles and turned her head back and forth at each verbal exchange between the handsome man with the red car and the beautiful red-haired woman next to her.

"My name is Bert. What's your name, Red?"

"Not red! You silly. My name is Sarah Lou."

"Can I offer you a ride, Sarah Lou?"

She jumped off the bench and into the Porsche so fast she almost ripped the door off its hinges. As Bert and his new conquest drove away, Audry shaded her eyes and put a hand on her hip; she still had a stern disapproving look. Mavis, however, was all smiles and waived good-by as the Porsche disappeared in traffic.

Audry said, "We're most likely the last people on earth to see that young girl alive. He looked like a serial killer to me!"

Mavis said, "If I were as young as she is and looked as good, it would be me in that red wagon, and when I was through with the handsome devil he would never want another woman."

Audry was shocked. "Mavis! You're nothing but a dirty old woman. Is sex all you ever think about?"

"Is there something better?"

Jack was puffing when he reached his corner at Twelfth and Ash. He stopped briefly and before continuing, pondered why someone like Bert, an Attorney, would want to become friends. Jack felt, that he and Bert lived in two different worlds. The only things they had in common were jogging and beautiful women.

Shaking the incident from his mind, he sprinted around the corner, and up Ash, the street he lived on. As the old house he was buying came into view, he admired his handiwork--the green shutters, open permanently at the sides of the windows. The covered porch and railing painted white. A vine covered trellis enclosed one side and the end. His pride and joy were the rose bushes lining both sides of the steps below the porch railing. Their scent was in the air.

He thought, 'Their colors really dress up the place.'

The money Jack saved from photo assignments went into a special account. He had almost enough saved to pay off the old house and fix it up the way he wanted.

Mrs. Lola Bobolinsky, his next door neighbor, was working in her garden. Jack waved as he jogged passed.

"Hi Lola."

"Hello Jack. I see you are still jigging."

"That's jogging, Mrs. B."

"Jogging, smogging," she mumbled to herself. "Your roses are growing well; I can smell them from here." She waved at him with a garden tool and shouted, "I'll be over to clean later."

"You cleaned yesterday," he shouted back.

"But I might have missed something!"

Jack didn't dare stop. If he did, he was sure to receive an unwanted lecture about his health. She constantly told him he looked peaked.

*   *   *

A few days later, Jack called Bert and they agreed to meet at a new sports bar and grill in downtown Phoenix. Jack was surprised when Bert showed up with Sarah Lou, the red-headed speed walker from the park. Jack brought Jill Morra as his date. He had met her some weeks before at a faculty party. They were introduced because of their names, and their friends made good-natured fun of them. It was an embarrassment to them both. Although Jack disliked being in this position, if their names hadn't been linked with a stupid nursery rime, he might never have met Jill. Since that party, she had become a major part of his life. At first, Jill, who was secretary to the Dean of Women, showed no interest in Jack. It was obvious to everyone, except Jack, that she was trying to avoid him, but when someone mentioned how good Jack's photo work was, she offered to pose for him. As it turned out, posing in the nude was a turn-on for her, and they spent as much time in bed as they did taking photos. One thing led to another. He fell in love with her, and he assumed she was in love with him. It was her suggestion they live together.

*   *   *

On another day, he jogged up his front walk and stopped at the porch steps to catch his breath.

Focus, who had been waiting on the porch rail, jumped down to greet him. Jack talked to her often, as if she were a person, and she understood every word. But just so he wouldn't get the wrong idea, she remained loyal to the universally aloof cat attitude and acted as if she understood nothing. It was beyond her why humans could not hear her mind voice as she did theirs, but she kept trying, with Jack anyway.

'Meow, Jack. Did you have a nice jog?'

He picked her up, held her to his shoulder, stroked her, then sat on the top step. She instinctively knew what he was going to say--he was going to tell her about the money he had saved to buy the house. Focus had heard this story so many times, she grew tired of hearing it. "Cat, I've saved almost enough money to buy this old house, and when I do, I'll fix it up to look like new.

It's a good thing you can't talk, because I want to surprise Jill."

'But Jack! I do talk. You just won't hear me. If you did I'd tell you not to trust her. She could care less about you, or your house. She's using you. You're nothing but a sex object to her.'

Focus followed Jack into the house. He was always

courteous and held the door open until she was in. He was eager to share the news about the house and called out Jill's name. She was not in the bedroom or the kitchen.

He thought, 'She must have already gone to work.'

'I could have told you that,' thought Focus.

*   *   *

Several jogs later, Jack had finished his shower and dressed. He was ready to grab something to eat and leave for the college. Now normally, Jill should have already left, but this morning she was behind schedule and Jack saw this as an opportunity to tell her about the house money.

Jill had long dark brown hair--she had a slight resemblance to Elizabeth Taylor, at least she had been told she did. She had a terrific face and a body to go with it. Jill was stacked and she knew it, and Jack was in love with her. She was admiring herself in the full length hall mirror, and giving her makeup a final check, when Jack came up behind her and put his arms around her.

"Don't! Jack. You'll muss my hair," he saw her frown in the mirror and let her go. "I just wanted to tell you about something special." His voice sounded eager.

Hers sounded condescending. "Oh, really. What's that."

"I think I've saved enough money to pay off the house. Isn't that great?"

Jill looked at him as if he had lost his mind.

"Are you serious? You would actually buy this relic. I hoped you had given up on that idea."

He tried to take her into his arms again, but she eluded his advances.

"No, I still plan to buy it. It's a well built old house; there's not a crack in it. It has enough room to raise a family, and we could . . .."

84

"Jack! You must understand. I have no plans or desire to get married or have children." She softened her voice and took his face between her hands. "Why can't you be content with the way things are? You know how it turns me on to pose nude for you, and the sex after is terrific."

Jack was disappointed and stepped back from her.

"I suppose you're right--I just felt after all our time together, you might have changed your mind." She kissed at his mouth and missed. "Sorry. I have to leave. I'll see you later."

TWO

Jack had just finished drying the black and white pictures he had selected as his best examples for submission to the editor of Autumn Life Magazine. He spread them out on the work table and checked them over very carefully with his eye loop. To qualify for submission, each photograph had to be perfect in his eyes, and Jack was very pleased with the results. Focus jumped up onto the table and sat next to the display. 'Don't worry I'll make sure I don't touch anything--you're so fussy, always afraid I might leave a hair on a picture."

When Jill was not in the house, Jack usually talked to the cat. Sometimes, when Jill was there and Focus jumped onto his lap, he would talk to her, forgetting how annoyed it made Jill. She would tell him, "In my opinion, people who talk to animals are stupid and childish." This attitude annoyed the hell out of Jack, so he talked to Focus anyway, just to bug Jill.

"Well? What do you think, cat? Are they great character studies or what? If the editor doesn't like these examples, then he isn't going to like anything I show him."

'I think they're superb,' thought Focus. 'If they reject these, it will be their loss, but then what do I know, I'm only a cat.' Focus reached out a paw and touched a picture. 'I like this one the most.'

"Focus! Don't touch! Now get off the table!"

She put her ears back, jumped to the floor and left the room.

'Fussy, fussy.'

As Jack started to put his photo selections in order and attach their story sheets, the phone rang.

"Hello!"

"Simple Simon calling."

"Hi! Bert, haven't heard from you in awhile. What have you been doing with yourself?" he held the phone to his ear with his shoulder and continued to work.

"I broke up with Sarah Lou. She turned out to be a real air head, and you wouldn't believe her sloppy living habits. The apartment stayed in a mess most of the time and it didn't seem to bother her at all. She wouldn't even pick up her own things, let alone mine, and forget about cleaning up after dinner, I ended up doing that. She quit cooking altogether and we started eating out damn near every night. But when she insisted I get her a house keeper, that was the last straw. She even wanted me to hire Mrs. Bobo away from you. I had a hell of a time convincing her that Mrs. B, didn't hire out. I do have to admit, Sarah was great in bed, but I want more then good sex from a woman."

"Sure you do Bert."

"Well, it sounds good anyway."

"So? What are you going to do?"

"I'm moving out, and Sarah is going to keep the apartment."

Sometimes, Jack suffered from a malady called: slow-brain-quick mouth syndrome, and before giving himself a chance to think. He said, "Why don't you move into my spare bedroom and share the living expenses?"

Bert jumped at the offer.   "That's a terrific idea. How about tomorrow?"

"Okay! See you then."

Focus overheard the conversation.   'That was a dumb idea Jack.   This guy is a genuine self-centered phony.'

On a Saturday night, Jill, Jack, and Bert were lounging around, watching TV. Focus slept curled up in Jack's lap. They looked like three bored people.   Jill cuddled next to Jack on the couch. She had on shorts, a halter top, and was braless; her eyes were on the TV but her mind was elsewhere. *Bert is a handsome devil . . . I wonder if he fantasizes about me like I do him . . . I've caught him checking my dimensions more than once tonight . . . his lustful looks are making me hot.'*

Bert was stretched out in a lounge chair next to the couch with his feet on the foot stool. He had no idea what the movie was about.

He thought,   *'I know Jill is aware of my glances. She squirms every time I look at her fantastic body--she makes Sarah Lou look like a boy--I should concentrate on the movie, or leave the room--she's beginning to arouse me. Jack, you are one lucky dude.'*

Jack tried to ignore the obvious, but he would have had to be stupid and blind not to see what was, going on between his best friend and Jill. He thought *'I can only hope they don't succumb to their animal instincts and jump each other right here in front of me.   The way they're acting, I'm afraid to leave the room.'*

The heated atmosphere changed when Bert said.

"Do you people realize I've been here a week already, and the three of us haven't done anything together, except sit around and watch the boob tube."

Jack perked up at this comment.

"You're right, we should do something. We could go bowling! I used to be a pretty good bowler when I was in a league; I even had a two-eighty-nine game once."

"What a boring idea." said Jill, "I hate bowling,".

"How about horse back riding?" suggested Bert.

"That's it!" exclaimed Jill. "I love to ride!" Then she smiled at Jack and thought, *'Next to posing in the nude, riding a horse turns me on the most!'*

Unpleasant past encounters with horses welled up in Jack's memory, especially the time he was with his friends from school. Most of them had been on a horse before. Jack had not, and his horse threw him before they even left the corral. He decided long ago that he and horses did not belong together.

"I hate and despise horses and they know it. If you don't mind, let's think of something else."

Jill was very disappointed. "Oh! Jack, you're such a spoilsport. Please! Let's go."

Once again, Jack's mouth was faster than his mind. "If you want to go that bad, why don't you go with Bert? I don't mind, I have plenty to keep me busy here." The second after the words fell out of his mouth, he had second thoughts, *'What the hell, Bert's my best friend. He wouldn't try anything funny with Jill-- or would he?'*

The following Sunday, Mavis and Audry, who lived across the street from Jack, sat on their screened-in front porch checking the neighborhood activities. They knew so much about what went on around them, they could have put out a news letter.

From the day Bert moved into Jack's house, Audry recognized him as the man at the bus stop that had picked up the red-haired girl named Sarah Lou. As a result of that recognition, the two ladies spent more time than they normally did on the porch. Audry was knitting something, but she couldn't remember if it was a sweater or a scarf. It didn't matter, she just liked to knit.

Mavis had been reading a lusty romance novel for a month, and she was only half way through the book. If she didn't look up every time a car drove by, or someone walked by, or rode by on a bike, she would have finished the book long ago. Although he couldn't see them behind the porch screen, the evening paper boy knew they were there, and watching. He always made sure he hit the screen door when he threw the paper. He knew they were there for certain when Mavis yelled at him. "That was a good shot Bill!" whereas, without missing a stitch, Audry yelled, "You don't have to do that you know!"

"Look, Audry, something's going on at Jack's house. There goes that handsome devil, Bert with Jack's girlfriend, and they're getting into that pretty car. I wish I were her." Against her better judgment, Audry took a quick look.

"He still looks like a serial killer to me."

Jack watched from the porch as Jill and Bert climbed into the Porsche and drove away. He waved at the departing car, but they didn't see him. Focus jumped up onto the porch-rail and Jack absently stroked her.

"There go my two best pals, Focus. It's a lucky man who has two trustworthy friends to share his life with."

Focus looked up at him and wished with every ounce of her energy that Jack could hear her voice.

"You're the best human I know, and I care for you, but you're not too bright, are you? I wouldn't trust either of them as far as I could spit a fur ball!"

Along the park riding trail, Jill challenged Bert to a race. Laughing, and enjoying their outing, they raced until the horses were winded. Bert slowed his mount to a gallop and then to a walk. Jill followed.

"Let's stop in the shade of that tree ahead and cool off. I'm getting sweaty." As she said this, Jill unbuttoned her blouse all the way to her belly button. This all but uncovered her ample breasts. Bert did not fail to notice.

Once engulfed by the shade, Bert brought his horse to a halt, swung his right leg expertly over the saddle, dropped to the ground and flipped his reins over a low hanging branch. He took Jill's reins and did the same. Meanwhile, Jill had turned sideways in her saddle and using her 'helpless-female-voice,' said, "Bert, will you help me down." She smiled sweetly as she reached both hands toward him.

Bert, in his best impression of a western drawl said. "Be happy to ma'am," and took her hands in his. Jill slid from the saddle, slowly and closely down his front, putting her arms around his neck on the way. When her feet touched ground, they kissed longingly and tasted the heated passion that had drawn them together. There was no stopping them now. They ran, hand in hand, Jill leading, to a grassy spot behind thick bushes that concealed their activities. Then in a button-popping, zipper-ripping rush, they stripped their clothes off, threw them into a pile and used them as their bed of lust.

Short minutes later the two rapid rabbits walked quickly from their love nest, each checking belts, buttons, and zippers to make sure they were in place. The silence between them was strained, broken only by the wind in the trees, singing birds and horsey noises. They mounted up. It was no surprise to Bert that Jill needed no help getting back on her horse. As they trotted along toward the stables, neither knew what to say to the other.

In the Porsche on the way home, Jill smirked with satisfaction as she recalled their quickie in the park, but as they got closer to Jack's house, she changed her smirk to a phony pout.

"We should never have done that--it was so unfair to Jack."

Bert had a conqueror's smirk on his face, but when Jill expressed her feelings, he frowned in false remorse as visions of a repeat performance grew dim.

"You're right--I betrayed my best friend, I'm a traitor. We should never be alone together, ever again."

They parked the Porsche in the driveway and entered the house through the kitchen side door. Bert got a beer and sat at the table. Jill went into the bedroom and found a note from Jack taped on the bathroom mirror:

Jill, have gone to town. I'll be back around three.
Love, Jack.

Her mind switched immediately to Bert, and she unbuttoned her blouse. That lustful feeling for him returned. Looking in the mirror she caressed her breasts in ecstasy, then controlling her emotions, she buttoned her blouse.

"Get hold of yourself girl, you can't let your lust lead you astray again. I'll lock the door and stay in here until Jack gets home." But when Jill touched the handle, she turned it, flung the door wide and walked quickly into the kitchen. Bert looked up from his beer and saw she was flushed and trembling.

"Where's Jack?"

"He left a note; ah-he-he's gone to town," she stammered, "He won't be back until three," they both checked the kitchen clock. "It's only one thirty," said Bert. He stood, and stepped around the table toward Jill. She charged into his waiting arms, and sighed.

"Oh! Bert! Take me again."

Those words and actions started a fast four handed game of body groping and heated lustful-kissing, followed by a headlong rush to Bert's bedroom. They left the traditional trail of clothes scattered from the kitchen on down the hall.

During this lustful display of emotion, Focus had been sitting on the kitchen counter watching the peculiar antics of Jill and Bert. When the lovers were out of sight, the cat thought, 'Humans are strange creatures--they have to hide to have sex--when Jack gets home, there's going to be trouble in Phoenix city tonight.'

Ten minutes later, Jack walked into the kitchen, retrieved a cold beer from the fridge, opened it and took a swig. When he turned around, he noticed a single beer bottle on the table. Something about it bothered him, but he wasn't sure what it was and put it out of his mind.

"I'm sure they're here; Bert's car is parked in the side driveway. They must be in the living room." Jack walked briskly into the front room entry. Expecting to see Jill and Bert, he smiled, and was ready to ask how their horse back ride went.

No one was there, so he went back into the kitchen. His smile left him and was replaced by a frown. Jack leaned against the counter where Focus sat. She rubbed against him while he scratched her neck and rubbed her ears. "I can hardly wait to tell them the good news. Where could they be?"

THREE

He had to tell someone, so he told the cat.

"Guess what, cat? Just after Jill and Bert left, I had a call from the editor of Autumn Life magazine--he gave me the assignment. Won't Jill be surprised?"

'I'm sure she will, Jack, but guess what your two best friends are doing in the bedroom.'

As Jack finished a pull on his beer, his gaze fixed on the half empty bottle on the kitchen table. It looked out of place and left a wet ring when he picked it up. "*I have never known Jill or Bert to leave an unfinished beer. It's still cold, so it couldn't have been there long.*" Jack frowned as he fit the bottom of the bottle back into the wet ring. He drank again from his bottle, and the brew fizzed away in his mouth. As he lowered the bottle, two shoes on the floor caught his eye. One was Bert's, one was Jill's. A knot formed in the pit of his stomach. The blood drained from his face.

"Why do I have the feeling that my worst fears are about to come true?"

In the hall, just past those shoes, were their mates, and scattered randomly beyond were socks, a shirt, a blouse, and two pairs of pants. Jack's brain and body began to numb as the knot in his stomach expanded. The story these scattered clothes told was a truth he did not want to know. *"Tell me this doesn't mean what I think it does."*

'I'm sorry to tell you this, Jack, but it means exactly what you think it does, and from the look on your face, I would say the party is about over for those two. I hope they enjoyed their romp.'

Jack picked up clothes as he followed the marked trail to Bert's door, arriving there in time to hear the last gasps of spent passions from the two lovers. When Jack saw them on the bed, he shouted as loud as he could.

"What-have-you-done!" and heaved their clothes onto them. Jill screamed and they came apart like two scalded dogs. As they scrambled to cover themselves, the scene took on a comical air, but Jack was far from in a humorous mood and continued his shouting barrage.

"How long has this been going on? You both had me completely fooled. Jill, all this time I believed you really loved me, and Bert, you dirty-rotten-bastard. I trusted you; you had me convinced I was your best friend. What a damn dumb fool I've been!"

Jack seethed with hatred. Jill and Bert cowered wide eyed and kneeling on the bed.

"Both of you deceiving jerks get your things together and get the hell out of my house!"

Bert Simon, the lawyer, spoke up.

"Now, Jack. You just hold on a minute; my rent is paid to the end of the month and I'm not leaving."

Bert looked at Jill for support of his statement. She smirked at Jack and nodded her head in agreement. Jack turned the color of hot lead, gritted his teeth, and snarled at them.

"You just think you're not leaving!" he stood rigidly. His hands made into fists at his side. He was in such a red-rage he couldn't think straight.

"I'm going to leave you two lovers alone to decide your fate. If I stay in here and look at you for another second, I might lose all control and strangle both of you. You're lucky I don't have a gun! Now, let's see if you can get dressed as fast as you got undressed."

From the hallway, Focus thought. 'Give um hell Jack! Throw them out of my house. They're no more than trash.'

His rage still with him, he slammed their door and stormed down the hall to the refuge of his darkroom, but before going in, he shouted back at them.

"I-will-never-forgive-you-for-this!"

He entered his photo lab and slammed that door too. Jack was angrier than he could ever remember being in his entire life. So angry, his body shook. Feeling totally out of control, he knew he had to curb the venomous rush of adrenaline that was consuming him. He jerked the darkroom refrigerator door open.

Through clinched teeth he mumbled, "Maybe a V-8 will cool my brain."

The cold juice can was soothing as it touched his lips. He sloshed the juice into his mouth but abruptly stopped the flow with his tongue; the juice tasted spoiled and moldy. Gagging, he spit it into the sink and rinsed out his mouth. The moldy taste remained. There were other cans inside in the same condition.

On the wall next to the sink, a display of nude photos featuring Jill reminded him of past pleasures with her. Her smiling face mocked him. He sloshed the remainder of the moldy blood-red juice across the display.

Further venting his wrath, he shouted, "Smile now! You two-timing-bitch!" Hoping the sound of his voice would carry to her, he continued, "How could I have been so naive, so stupid?" His anger, still at its peak, he threw the empty can. It bounced off her picture. He roared like a wounded beast, and slammed the door shut so hard the refrigerator bounced against the wall and cracked the plaster. The impact hurled everything crashing together into a glass shattering liquid mass. The white box rocked back to level with a thump.

Jack felt much better, but thought, 'I'm not about to open that door. I've got a fair idea what it looks like; one big primordial pool of muck.'

Focus heard the rumpus and the shouting coming from the darkroom. She was glad she had waited in the hall.

'I never knew he could muster that much anger--I think it best I stay out of his way.'

Jack's bruised ego demanded revenge and he stomped out of the lab. His heavy foot falls made the wooden floor sound like a giant drum head. Jack locked the darkroom door, then stomped to Bert's door, and paused. A ridiculous scene popped into his mind.

"I always wanted to do this. It's my door and by damn I'm going to do it." Jack imagined a picture of Bert's face next to the door knob. With a mighty karate shout he kicked the door open. Jill and Bert were dressed and sitting on the edge of the bed. They were consoling each other when the door suddenly swung violently toward them. Jill screamed. Bert shouted. Jack faked a threatening lunge toward them and laughed like a madman. Jill screamed again and the two lovers dove over the far side of the bed. "Are you nuts?" shouted Bert, "I know you have every right to be angry, but you must try to calm yourself."

Jack tried to sound insane when he answered Bert.

"If you want to find out how nuts I really am, just-be-here-when-I-get-back!" He laughed insanely, turned dramatically, and left the room. Focus trotted along beside him.

'That was a three-meow performance Jack. It's too bad you can't hear me, I could have told you this was going to happen.'

Jack's anger level was much lower, but still there. Focus followed him out the front door. He almost slammed it as a parting gesture, but stopped himself.

"I won't slam this one Focus--vintage glass doors are difficult to replace. I'm going for a jog. I have to get away from here for a while--maybe those pals of mine will be gone when I get back." He launched into a power sprint toward the park, and the cat's mind words trailed after him.

'Good self control, Jack. I'll wait for you here, I don't care for jogging. Besides, it's time for my next nap.'

Jack had to slow his hard driving pace to a fast walk. Winded more than usual, he stopped in the shade. A light headed feeling caught him off guard. He had trouble catching his breath, but his anger was now subdued--less intense. A man from a nearby park bench spoke to him.

"Why don't you take a breather and sit before you collapse?"

"Thanks!" he gasped. "I think I will." The extra energy he had forced into his power sprint was exhausting. He sat with a plop, stretched out his legs and put his elbows on the top of the back rest. His heart beat harder than normal and fear of a stroke entered his mind, but in a few seconds his heart rate slowed and his breathing returned to normal. He felt fine. The man on the other end of the bench watched him.

"You had me worried. For a minute there you didn't look too good. I was afraid I might have to call 911."

The man, in his late fifties, looked fit. He wore a western hat, a western suit, a Bola tie and cowboy boots.

"You seem to have a troubled mind. Is that what brought on this race with yourself? If you could use a sympathetic ear from a stranger, I'm a good listener."

Jack sized the man up again and figured he had nothing to lose by telling him what happened. After all, they were not likely to meet again.

"It's very personal, I don't normally talk to strangers about my love life--but what the hell. The way I feel right now I'd like to stand on a soap box and gather a crowd."

He mulled over what had occurred just a short time ago, then started telling the stranger about his friends deceit.

"What happened was, just a few minutes ago, I caught my lady friend and my so called best friend in bed making out." Jack saw no adverse reaction from the man and continued his story.

"I've never had the urge to commit mayhem or murder, but at that moment, I was very close. I still feel angry enough to go back and strangle them, dismember their bodies and throw their parts out with the garbage, but I guess I couldn't really do that--too messy; besides, what would the neighbors think?"

The western man smiled, but made no comment; however, Jack's words triggered his overactive imagination and he pictured himself on his front porch dismantling two mannequins. The female mannequin had the name, "Jill" stamped in bold black letters on its forehead and on all of the individual body parts. The male mannequin had "Bert" stamped all over it. Jack saw this sceen in stop motion, like an old flickering silent movie.

Now, in fast motion, he stuffed all the body parts into plastic garbage bags, carried them to the street curb, and set them down. Then he put his hands above his head showing the "V for victory" sign to his neighbors. They all gathered around clapping and cheering. A garbage truck rolled to a stop and Jack threw the bags of body parts into the back. As it pulled away, Jack and the crowd waved good-by.

The western man gently shook Jack's shoulder and Jack came out of his dream state.

"I don't know what you were dreaming about, but whatever it was, from the expression on your face, it was a pleasant experience."

"It was, but it won't solve my problem."

Jack stood, shook the tightness from his arms and legs and did a couple of stretching moves off the bench. A mental picture of clothes scattered on the floor popped into his mind, and the anger was suddenly back.

"Screw them both! I'm going back and kick their hot butts out of my house!"

He shook the man's hand. "Thanks for listening to my ravings."

Jack turned to leave, but the western man raised his hand, showing he wanted to say something.

"If I could have a minute of your time before you leave. Because of your frame of mind, I think I should introduce myself. I'm John Good, Chief of Homicide. I retired last week from the Phoenix P.D. and I offer you this friendly advice; be very careful what you say to strangers. I wouldn't want to read about your arrest in the papers."

Jack's mouth was open in surprise. He closed it and said, "I can assure you, chief, my talk is bigger than my actions. Thanks again for listening. It really did help." He shook the chief's hand again, then slow-jogged home.

FOUR

When Jack reached his corner, he was stopped by a strange scene. Random groups of people from the neighborhood were gathered in the street and on the sidewalk near his house. A few had their faces covered with handkerchiefs, some with gas masks. Others wore paper dentist masks.

As soon as he walked around the corner, he heard muffled angry voices, and for reasons unknown to Jack, their anger was directed at him.

Uncertain what was going on, and not sure he wanted to find out, he continued walking. He saw Mrs. Bobo working in her garden and wearing an air filter. She waved at Jack, her shout muffled by the filter.

"I'll be over to clean when the smell is gone."

"You cleaned yesterday," he shouted back.

One step more and he got a full whiff of an awful smell. His eyes watered instantly. Now he understood the reason for all the air-filters. Jack grabbed his handkerchief, mimicking his neighbors. "What a rotten odor!" exclaimed Jack. "I wonder where it's coming from?"

He looked around for an answer to his question. Before he could turn into his front walk, a man he had never seen before stepped in front of him, folded his arms, planted himself feet spread, and blocked Jack's progress. The stranger wore a World-War-One gas mask.

Jack felt the need for the same filter protection, not so much from the pungent odor in the air, but from the man's boozy breath, which now dominated Jack's air space.

Mr. Whisky Breath shook his fist in Jack's face.

"You better do something about this poison gas!"

"What are you talking about? I don't know anything about this. Besides, if it were poison gas, you would be dead and so would I. Now move!"

"Mr.! I ain't sure what you been up to in there, and by damn I ain't going to stand around waiting to find out. I called the cops!"

"You did what?"

"I called the cops."

"Get out of my way!" He tried to shove Mr. booze-breath out of the way, in an attempt to walk around him, but the man recovered his balance and grabbed hold of Jack's belt from behind. Jack dragged the man a few feet before he could shake him off.

"Are you nuts? Get away from me!" He shoved the drunk away again.

Just as Jack reached the bottom step, a police cruiser, siren blaring, careened around the corner and screeched to a skidding halt in front of his house. Two cops jumped out, their hands poised near their weapons. The gas-mask drunk staggered over to them and pointed at Jack.

"That's him! That's the guy! Arrest the murderer! He tried to kill me!"

Jack looked disgusted. "Wait a minute! This guy is drunk and he . . ."

The first cop cut Jack off. "Hold it! Which one of you called to report a dead body?"

Jack was amazed. "Dead body! There's no dead body! This man has made a mistake and I can . ."

The second cop cut him off this time.

"If you didn't make the call, then it must be this man. Did you call 911?"

"You're damn right! And I bet my wife there's a body laying right there in the middle of his front room."

Jack started down the steps. "This is crazy, I can prove . . ."

"You! Stop right there and keep your hands where we can see them." While this was going on, Jack's masked neighbors had gathered behind the patrol car. They didn't want to miss a thing.

"Did you hear that Audrey?" said Mavis. "Jack murdered his roommate!"

"Well I'm not surprised," said Audrey. "The three of them living in sin like that."

"Please! Listen to me, this is getting way out of control." Focus waited on the porch rail, taking in these strange human activities.

'If they could hear me, I would straighten this out in two shakes of my tail.'

"If you will just come up on the porch, I'll tell you where the smell is coming from. It's not serious and there is no dead body."

Gas-mask man said. "I'm coming with yah. I want to see what's in there."

"Mister! We can handle this without your help."

"But he tried to kill me!"

"We saw what happened, and it was nothing. Now you go home and sober up or we will arrest you for disturbing the peace."

The gas-masked man staggered down the sidewalk mumbling about his rights. Jack waited on the porch for the cops, but when they entered the 'Smelling Zone' the odor stopped them in their tracks. Their handkerchiefs came out to wipe away their sudden tears. They backed away gagging. It took all the willpower they had not to barf.

Still backing away Jack followed them and attempted to explain.

"Don't come any closer. Stay right where you are. One thing is for sure," said Sergeant Turkel. "That can't be a dead body, it smells too bad."

"The reason it smells so bad is, I spilled some chemicals in my darkroom, and they accidentally mixed, causing this odor."

Both cops still choked and gagged, and their color changed from beet-red to that of chalk-faced Zombie's. As they backed toward their patrol car, officer Turkel had parting words.

"Mister Stump, I want you to understand this. Either you get rid of this putrid odor yourself, or we'll come back with a hazardous waste team to clean it up for you at your expense, plus penalties. If you don't clean it up, I personally will see that you spend time in a cell!" Turkel was shouting now.

"Do you understand me?"

"Yes! Yes! I understand."

The cops were eager to leave, posthaste. After piling awkwardly into their cruiser, they roared down the street, trying to outdistance the odor. After the cops left, Jack addressed his neighbors.

"Thanks so very much for coming; you've been grand, but now the show is over, so why don't you good people go crawl back into your holes? As he walked up the porch steps, the odor became stronger and he began to understand why all these angry people held him responsible. Focus waited for him on the top step.

'Smell the exotic perfume,' she thought to Jack. 'It's more fragrant than your roses--I see you're still in a bad mood. Breath deep, the sweet air will make you feel better.'

The front door was locked. He expected it to be unlocked when he returned. Naturally he suspected Jill or Bert had locked him out of the house.

"Very funny, Jill!" Jack shouted. "Now unlock the stupid door!" He pounded on the door until it rattled, then stopped pounding when he noticed a small yellow piece of paper stuck to a glass pane. It was a note written in Bert's pinched small handwriting. He peeled it off the glass.

"What now?" Jack doubled his handkerchief and hoped it would keep out the eye stinging vapors. His watery eyes made the note difficult to read. He walked to the porch rail, held the note in the brighter light, and read it aloud.

"Jack, the smell in the house is so bad it made us sick and we had to leave. We tried to find the source, but couldn't. Maybe you can . . . Bert and Jill."

"Well up yours!" said Jack. He wadded the note into a small ball then with his thumb flipped it off the porch. "I wonder if that old pass key is still on the molding above the door." He felt along the ledge, but failed to produce a key, so he banged on the door out of frustration.

The pounding dislodged the key. It slid off the ledge and bounced off his bald spot.

"Damn! That hurt." He rubbed the top of his head and looked to the heavens. "Thanks! I needed that."

After unlocking the door, he pushed it open cautiously, just a crack, and a green cloud of vapor seeped out like fog from around the door. The odor was so strong and penetrating; his handkerchief was useless. He staggered back to the porch rail so fast, it appeared as if someone in the house had caught him with an uppercut. The green vapor dissipated quickly and left Jack choking and gagging.

'On the other hand,' thought Focus, 'Isn't that a wonderful smell?'

Jack mustered all his courage, held his cloth face mask tight, reached out with his foot and shoved the door open all the way. More vapor escaped, but it was not as dense a cloud this time.

When the neighbors saw Jack open the door, and the green vapors escape, they held their face masks even tighter and retreated across the street. A few moments later they could see and hear windows all around the house being flung open. All except the windows in the dark room. They were painted black and sealed. He would have to go in there later. Next, he turned on a twenty-four-inch fan and set the swamp cooler on high. Seconds later, his neighbors saw him race through the open front door, down the steps, then drop to his knees gasping for air.

Focus rubbed against him. 'Jack, that delightful smelling vapor is coming from your darkroom.'

He picked the cat up and sat on the top step while he waited for the fans to do their job and for natural air to circulate through the house. It suddenly came to him where the odor was coming from.

"I know what's causing this problem Focus; the vapors must be coming from the darkroom! Remember? I slammed the refrigerator door and broke everything."

'Brilliant deduction, Jack.'

He put the cat down, covered his face and entered the house again. From the middle of the kitchen he could see vapors under pressure spurting randomly from under the darkroom door. He left quickly, deciding he might as well wait awhile to open that door. On the front porch, he had another thought, 'Maybe the smell will dissipate entirely in a few hours--meanwhile, I'll drive over to Fred Wong's and ask him to put me up for the night.'

Jack stopped his motor driven bucket of bolts in front of Fred's house and turned off the ignition. The engine backfired once, sounding as if a gun had been fired, then it belched dirty-gray-smoke from the exhaust pipe.

Fred Wong lived two blocks from Jack; he also worked at Phoenix College where he taught chemistry. Jack and he were good friends and had known each other for several years. Fred was the typical absent-minded professor type and would rather be doing research than teaching.

Jack rang Fred's door bell, and Fred opened the door. It only took a split second for the odor that had permeated Jack's clothing to assault Fred's senses.

"What the hell did you get into? Did you trip over a skunk? Wait! I don't care what happened,--you can't come in. You smell rank. Now go away!" said Fred. He closed the door abruptly in Jack's face. Jack rang the bell again.

"Go home and take a bath!" shouted Fred

"Please! Let me stay, Fred. I can't go back to my place tonight, the odor is worse there."

"Let me guess what happened: Your sewer backed up while you were taking a bath with your clothes on."

"Nothing that simple. I broke some chemical bottles in the darkroom, and their contents combined into something horrendous."

"Where are Jill and Bert?"

"I don't much care where they are. I caught them in bed making out."

"Are you serious? Jill and your best friend, Bert?" There was silence for a moment and Jack thought Fred had moved away from the door. He rapped lightly. "Fred--are you still there?"

Fred answered in a reluctant manner, "Yes. I'm still here. Okay, I'll take pity on you, but you still can't come in. There's a one-man tent and an old sleeping bag in the garage. Set yourself up in the back yard and I'll put something on the back porch for you to eat."

"I'll take it. Thanks buddy!"

Jack got the tent and sleeping bag and set up camp. He was so tired and emotionally strung out, it didn't matter to him where he slept. Fred came to the back porch with a tray of food and put it on the landing.

"Jack!" he called. "Here's your dinner. Damn, that smell is potent. Don't come over here until I'm back inside."

Fred closed the door and Jack started after the tray.

The dog next door had been watching Jack and smelled the food. The dog decided it might be something for him and came after it. Jack saw what it was up to.

"Hey! Get away from there. Shoo!"

Jack grabbed the tray, the dog grabbed Jack's pant leg by the cuff, but let go, began whining, and backed away. All the while whimpering and acting as if it were trying to get something most foul out of its mouth. Jack said, "Scat!", and kicked at the mutt. It ran home crying and making a fuss. The dog owner came out and saw his dog was in distress, then saw Jack standing there with the tray of food.

"Hey! You!" he shouted. "What did you do to my dog? You tried to poison him, didn't you? I'll fix your ass." He picked up a length of two-by-four and started for Jack. Jack backed up and was about to throw the food tray at him, but when the dog lover got close enough to smell Jack's odor, he stopped, gagged and dropped the board.

"Mister, I don't know what you fell into, but you smell bad. I mean you smell really bad." Then he and his dog ran for the safety of their house.

Jack shook his fist and shouted at the retreating pair. "Let that be a lesson to you and don't come back." He sat on the steps of the porch and ate his hard won meal. When he finished, he crawled into the sleeping bag and fell into welcome asleep.

FIVE

The next morning at first light, Jack awoke slowly from a strange, but pleasant dream. He dreamed he was at the mercy of several lustful women. They kissed his hands, his arms, his face, and his lips. Their combined loud purring sounded as if he were surrounded by a pride of lions.

He turned on his side and put his arm around one lovely and mumbled, "Not now ladies. I have to go to work," then his mind slipped into the next level of consciousness, and he opened his eyes to slits. The lovely he had his arm around licked his lips and purred. It was a white cat. He lifted his head and saw there were at least a dozen cats in the tent with him. They took no notice of his movement and continued their amorous licking and rubbing. Jack shouted. "Get out! Get out!"

Fred was standing on the porch about to call to Jack when Jack shouted. Fred witnessed the comical scene as cats of all descriptions and colors came flying out of the tent followed by Jack.

After Fred controlled his hysterical laughter, he said, "That's the funniest thing I've ever seen, but you should stop fooling around with those cats and go home. It's time for work." A couple of the cats came back and rubbed against Jack's legs; still drawn to his exotic odor. Others went back into the tent and lolled around on the sleeping bag. One lay on his shirt, another tried to crawl into his shoe. He had a tug of war trying pull his clothes away from them.

Finally, after dressing, he went out to his car and prepared to leave, but before he opened the door, he saw movement inside. A look through the open passenger side window revealed a car full of cats lounging in the ambrosia of cat heaven. He shook his head in disbelief and walked toward home two blocks away. Three cats followed him for half-a-block, then as a unit they stopped and hurried back to the car to indulge in their opiate.

From concealment behind a tree on the corner of his street, Jack checked up the street to see if there was a neighborhood welcoming committee or any cops waiting to arrest him. The street appeared deserted, so he walked swiftly the rest of the way home and into the house. His dulled senses told him the odorous vapors were gone. But from across the street:

"Audry."

"What, Mavis?"

"Jack's back."

"That's nice. Can I take off this mask now?"

Jack took a refreshing shower, changed clothes and had a bite to eat. The food tasted a little odd, but not bad. In his bedroom, Focus sat on top of the bureau and watched him brush his hair, then slip into a jacket.

"I can't detect that odor anymore. Maybe the vapors

have dissipated. I sure hope I'm right."

'You still have the fragrance on you, and it smells better than your after shave. Your friends at work will love you,' thought Focus.

After his walk to work Jack felt physically fit; but as he strolled down the hall toward his office, it was obvious he still had an odor problem. His friends allowed him plenty of room to pass and gave him dirty looks. Some even made insulting remarks:

"Jack! You're disgusting!"

"Have you joined the unwashed!"

"You have the worst case of BO in the world."

And, "Take a bath, Jack."

He thought, 'The vapors must have penetrated every crack, crevice and closet in the house.'

Down the hall a few feet ahead and opposite his office door, the college Dean greeted people with a smile and a handshake. When Jack approached him, the Dean's eyes watered, he looked nauseated, turned away, hurried into his office, and quickly closed his door. Jack went to his own office, but before he could close the door, the phone rang.

"Jack!" he shouted. "I don't know what your problem is, but that was the worst odor I have ever encountered in my entire life! I'm putting you on temporary leave. I want you to return home, at once! And don't come back until you have rid yourself of that odor." He hung up before Jack could explain.

"Okay! Okay! I'll leave. I know when I'm not wanted. I can take a hint," he said into the dead phone. Then he banged the phone down. "Unfriendly jerk--Damn! It will be a thankful day when I can leave here for good!"

On the walk home, Jack could not detect a scent coming from his clothes, but from the reaction and attention he received in the hall, his senses were obviously out of whack.

When he entered the house, the phone was ringing. Jack answered it angrily.

"Hello! Who is this?"

"Jack? This is Jill."

"So! What do you want?"

"You might as well know, I'm not coming back to you."

Jack laughed at her. "You sure as hell got that right."

"Do you have to be so nasty?"

"You bet I do. Get to the point. What do you want?"

"Well, Bert and I are coming over to pick up our things. We tried to get into the house while you were gone, but the smell was so awful we didn't go in."

"Ahh gee. That's too bad. I hope you both became deathly ill. You're the reason for this mess."

"That may be so, but Bert said to tell you we want our things replaced or we'll sue you for destruction of personal property."

Jack put on the friendliest, calmest, voice he could muster and said, "Jill?"

"Yes Jack."

"Can you hear me all right?"

"Yes."

"Good. Then why don't you and my old buddy Bert, GO STRAIGHT TO HELL! Jack didn't wait for a reply, but with a smile of satisfaction, dropped the phone onto its cradle.

Determined to finish the cleanup, he went to his bedroom and changed into comfortable clothes.

In the vicinity of the darkroom the fumes were not as strong as when he first encountered them. As far as his nose was concerned, they were nonexistent.

But, just in case the vapors were stronger than he had anticipated, he held his handkerchief tightly over his nose and mouth. Unsure of what he was about to face, he cautiously unlocked the darkroom door. Then he opened it enough to slip his hand in and feel for the light switch. He found it and turned on the hanging overhead lights.

Mustering even more courage, he pushed the door full open and jumped back. When nothing happened he stepped through the doorway and stopped. The odor was strong again.

The first thing that caught his eye was how the refrigerator had changed--it had taken on the form of a cartoon-like character. It looked stuffed and bulging and the sides puffed out; as if something had exploded inside.

He concluded the source of the odor could only be the dark-brown gunk that oozed slowly from a crack at the bottom of the refrigerator door. It crept like flowing lava as it pooled and bubbled on the floor.

Jack's instincts told him to retreat, bow to the enemy. Do not walk. Run to the nearest fresh air, but as desperately as he wanted to do just that, he knew he could not. He must tough it out and clean up this unusual mess.

Just then Ms. Focus strolled in, rubbed against his legs, sniffed the air, then trotted quickly to the muck. She took an exploratory lick and decided it was the most exotic thing she had ever tasted in this or any of her other eight lives and before Jack could stop her, she took a few hefty bites.

"Hey! You stupid cat! No! Stop that." He rushed to her, picked her up and put her in the hall. "How could you eat that stinking goo? It might be poison!"

Focus turned her ears back and cringed at Jack's verbal assault. Her irises widened and looked like two big black buttons.

She thought, 'You might be right, Jack. This stuff could be poison. If it is, what a way to go! I can't believe it's poison though--it smells and tastes wonderful. I do feel somewhat light headed--I think I need a nap. Jack? Now I feel very peculiar, as if my senses were sharpened to a fine point. Strangest of all, I not only hear your words when you speak, but your thoughts as well; this could be fun.'

"Sorry about the yelling, Focus," Jack reached down and stroked her head and back. She pressed her head against his strokes and looked at him with half-closed eyes. Contented and purring, she licked her chops.

Jack said, "If you like that stinking muck that much, why not bring in all your friends and have a feast. Eat it all. Then I won't have to clean it up," he immediately felt remorse about his verbal attack on the cat.

"Listen to me--now I'm taking it out on the cat. Strange, but she seemed to like the stuff, and I'm about to barf from the smell of it--although it doesn't smell as strong now as it did. The odor has either dissipated or I'm getting used to it again--in a pleasant way, the odor is making me light headed--I think I need a nap. How come the rotten smell doesn't bother you, cat?"

'What rotten smell?' thought Focus. 'It might smell bad to you, but then, you have no true gourmet's taste, such as I, and I think it tastes great!'

Purring, she looked up at Jack, then continued licking her paws and cleaning her face.

"I would swear I just heard a soft, sultry, melodious voice in my head. It said, 'What rotten smell--and then, something else."

'You did Jack. It was me--Focus. I'm so happy you can finally hear my thoughts.'

"Now I know I've lost it for sure. I just heard my cat talk in my head. Where's my guardian angel when I need her? Don't I have enough problems?"

Jack tried to put this new, surely-imagined event out of his mind and return his attention to the mess of the century. He was distracted again when he tried to form a plan for the big clean up. Like an old black and white ghost movie, the memory of how this mess was created played back in slow motion on the projection screen of his mind.

A ghost like image of himself appeared standing in front of the open refrigerator door--the light from within illuminating his face as he reached for an open can of V-8 juice. Each event appeared as it had happened; from where he sloshed the moldy juice across Jill's mocking pictures, then threw the empty can at her smiling face, to where he slammed the refrigerator door.

The result of that angry action was now seeping out onto the floor before him, and forming into a thick bubbling pool of primordial ooze.

Jack shook the memory from his mind. The stench had returned him to reality. His handkerchief helped a little but as tears streamed from his red, swollen eyes, he raised one hand to the heavens, his face pointed in the same direction, pleading.

"Oh great and wondrous Gods of Photography! Grant me one wish; give me a gas mask--please!"

SIX

When a gas mask didn't appear, he got a wet mop and tried to sop up the spreading molasses-like quagmire. He held his breath, then mopped as hard and fast as he could until he turned blue in the face. Then he dropped the mop handle, slapped his handkerchief back over his face and gasped air through it. The mop was ineffective and just spread the muck around.

He put the mop aside and with a dust pan tried to scoop it up. The dust pan was wobbly and the muck was heavy and slick and kept sliding off the pan. None of it went into the ready bucket, but while trying to pick it up, he got it all over his hands. The substance would not stick to the pan, but, unfortunatly for Jack, it stuck quite well to his skin.

While he went to the sink and tried to wash off the slippery slime, he tried to remember what he had stored in the bloated refrigerator besides four or five gallons of used film-fix. In addition to the film-fix, he remembered a container of black liquid rubber and its catalyst for making molds. A full carton of stale milk. A couple of partially eaten sandwiches in various stages of decay, and several bottles, whose contents were a mystery. Whatever was in them must have been important or he would not have saved them. Jack was a packrat.

At the sink, he worked up a good soapy lather, but when he rinsed his hands off they remained sticky. He tried again with the soap; the results were the same. "Hey Focus! The fans must be doing their job, the stink isn't as strong now."

'What stink?' thought Focus

"There's that voice again. It just said. "What stink?"

'You might as well get used to it Jack, because I can't keep you from hearing my thoughts.'

"Ok! Ok! I'll try to live with this, but I still find it hard to believe that I think I'm talking with my cat. I must have slipped a gear. That's it. The fumes from this muck are causing me to hallucinate."

Jack's frustrations increased as every attempt he made to lift the muck from the floor failed. But when he chopped at the edge of the muck puddle with the dustpan, a small amount broke off intact, solidified for a few seconds then turned liquid again. In a way it reminded Jack of some stuff called Silly-Putty that he had played with when he was a kid; the difference was, Silly-Putty didn't stick to your hands.

Disgusted at his lack of progress with the clean up, he spoke to Focus.

"I just wish Bert and Jill were here to join in the fun. It would give me enormous pleasure to shove their cheating, smug faces into this crap."

'I would love to see that,' answered Focus.

"Right now, if I had my way--I would close the darkroom door, lock it, then come back when this mess has dried up. And I would too, except the cops would come back and arrest me," he continued, "I think I know a way to get the muck off the floor and into a container, but before I do that, I have an urgent need to get this sticky ca-ca off my hands."

Although the stuff was on his hands, he felt as if he were suffocating, and that he had gloves on his hands. He went to the sink and washed them again.

The bulging muck-maker continued to pass gas, plop ominously, and sigh with relief.

"Damn! This stuff is sticky. I can't seem to get it all off!"

His hands felt strange, cold, airy, and tingly. They even looked strange. He held them up to the light over the sink.

"I'm getting another kind of reaction from this stuff. Besides allowing me to hear and converse with Focus--the skin on my hands and arms is moving--rippling."

His eyes went wide with fear and his mouth dropped open, but at the same time he was fascinated as he watched black hair sprout from the back of his hands.

"What!--What is this?" he shouted. "What's happening to me?"

Focus wondered what was going on with Jack and jumped up on the counter next to the sink to see for herself. Like Jack, she saw the hair grow slowly up his arms.

"This can't be!--I can't believe what I'm seeing!"

Then, like the action in stop-motion film, the hair grew faster.

"Focus!" he yelled, and held his arms toward her. "Look what's happening to me!" Focus jumped down from the counter and walked away.

'Don't get so excited, Jack. It's only hair.'

"But it's real hair!"

Jack turned back to the sink and frantically squirted liquid soap on his hands and arms, rapidly working up a lather everywhere there was hair. He then grabbed a fingernail scrub-brush, the kind doctors use, and scrubbed to no avail.

He stopped soaping himself and ran to the shower when he couldn't keep up with the speedy hair growth. He rinsed off, clothes and all, but it had no effect on the hair as it continued to spread. He took off his soaked clothes in the shower and left them there.

He tried to pull the new hair out but that was painful. Even with scissors, or barbers' clippers, he still couldn't cut it off fast enough; it just kept growing back.

"Come off! Please come off! What's happening to me?"

Jack was frantic. He stopped trying to remove the hair. Frustrated, and not knowing what else to do, he put both hands on top of his head.

"What can I do to stop this? I'm beginning to look like a walking hair-ball."

He removed his hands from his head. Seconds later, hair hung over his eyes.

"At least I'm not bald any more." He pushed the new hair up so he could see himself in the mirror; what he could see made him laugh hysterically.

"I've got to see this better!"

He ran into the front hall and slid to a stop in front of the full-length mirror. He froze like a posing mannequin when he saw the shaggy beast that looked back at him. Hair stuck out everywhere. Focus jumped onto the hall table next to the mirror.

'I think you're having a bad-hair day, Jack.'

"That's an understatement. I look like a Neanderthal--no--more like a chimp. This is impossible!" he shouted. Except for the oval of his face, his protruding ears, the palms of his hands andthe bottom of his feet, his entire body was covered with shiny black hair. He looked quickly behind himself, hoping the image he saw was someone else, then back to the mirror. He laughed wildly.

"No one else here but the cat and us monkeys, sooo it must be me."

Jack danced from one foot to the other, beat his chest and scratched under his arms while he mimicked his version of a monkey chant.

"Hu-hu-hu-he-he. I look like the Sun's Gorilla! I just can't believe this! On the other hand, I can't deny it either. It really is me under all this fur. "

Jack, you look much better with full body hair, but it's not as lovely as mine. Incidentally, if you want me to groom you, forget it. It's too big a job for me.

Jack stopped his antics and studied his reflection. He felt giddy.

"Focus! I know what I'll do! I'll audition for a stand-by job as the Sun's Gorilla!"

Jack dashed into his bedroom, put on his Sun's T-shirt, blue-jeans and jogging shoes. Focus stood on the edge of the table and looked after him. 'What is my human up to now?'

Jack came out of his bedroom dribbling a basketball. "What do you think, cat? Do I look like the Sun's mascot or what?"

'I think you have lost it. All this sudden hair has gone to your head, so to speak.'

Focus watched him run and dribble the ball through the kitchen, through the living room and back to the hall where he stopped and held the ball up ready to shoot at the waste basket next to the table where she sat. Jack rambled on as if he were a sports announcer.

"Hear the roar of the crowd. Jack Stump, the new Sun's Gorilla has the ball." Just then Jack's mind slipped into limbo-land and he imagined himself in the Sun's arena dribbling the ball down the court. As he dribbled, he imagined he heard the cheering crowd and a play by play of the game action by Al McCoy and Cotton Fitzsimmons.

"He shoots! . . . Shazam! Swisharue! For! Two! and Stump is fouled; the game is tied 101 to 101 . . . four seconds remain on time-out."

"You know Al, signing Jack Stump for this exhibition game between the Sun's and the Sun Devil's of ASU was a brilliant move by Coach Westphal."

"It sure was, Cotton. We taped an interview with Coach Westphal just before the game and I asked him about Jack Stump."

As the limbo-land dream played on in Jack's mind, he saw Coach Westphal, microphone in hand. In the background, Jack, as the gorilla, shot practice baskets. The Coach turned to face the camera.

"Al, we've all heard about Jack Stump, the man with too much hair and as you know, all the proceeds from tonight's game will go to Jack for the study of his unique hair problem. He has to shave his entire body twice a day; if he fails to do this, his hair grows so fast and long he trips over it. Incidentally, all his excess hair is donated to the Salvation Army; they use it to stuff pillows for the homeless."

"Thanks, Coach, for that insight on a wonderful humanitarian, Jack Stump. This is Al McCoy with Cotton Fitzsommons and we're back in play at the Sun's Arena. Four seconds remain on the game clock. Jack must make this basket to win the game."

Jack saw himself at the free-throw line. He bounced the ball a few times, then raised it to shoot.

"It's a breathless moment, Al."

"Yes it is Cotton . . .the ball is up! . . "

Jack's mind slipped back to reality and he shot the ball. It crashed off the rim of the waste-basket, dumped it over and spilled its contents across the floor.

"Damn! I should've made that one."

All the racket spooked Focus. She let out a howl, sprang straight up and off the table.

'I'm getting out of here! That hairy beast tried to hit me with a basketball.'

Jack set the basket upright and put the trash back in. As he picked up the ball he wondered what to do about his hairy condition. He felt as if he were in shock. He needed to lie down, to sleep, then awake to find it was all an unbelievable nightmare.

As he walked toward his bedroom, a knock at the front door startled him. He tucked the ball under his arm, and stuck his head around the hall corner to see who knocked. Even through the sheer drape over the front door window, there was no mistaking the figure standing there. It was Mrs. Lola Bobolinsky, his cleaning lady.

He whispered loudly. "Quick! Focus! Block the door. I can't let her see me like this! I'll scare the wits out of her."

'You don't scare me. You won't scare her. Come in Mrs. Bobo.'

"She can't hear you, can she?" he whispered again.

'I'm not sure, but we'll know in a minute.'

SEVEN

Lola was about to knock again, but hesitated when she heard a female voice she did not recognize. The voice caught her off guard when it invited her to come into the house. It confused her because she could not decide whether she heard the voice coming from the house, or in her mind.

It reminded Lola of the first time she heard a voice speak in her mind. It had taken place next to the ancient old shade oak at the edge of the family farm. At the time she was a senior in high school.

After getting off the school bus, it had been Lola's routine to stop in the shade of the tree, then from a hole in the trunk she would remove a dog-eared romance novel being passed around among her girl friends. Normally, she only had time to read two or three pages before heading for the house. This day was different. As Lola approached her private place, a voice spoke to her. It said, "You're late Lola,"

The voice itself sounded soft and gentle, but the very idea of hearing a voice in her mind frightened her.

Lola walked cautiously around the base of the enormous tree trunk, having no idea to whom the voice belonged, or from where it had come. When she saw no one, her thought was, 'I must have imagined I heard a voice--if I tell any of my friends about this, they'll think: 'Poor Lola has flipped her lid'.

Just as her confusion deepened, she felt the slobbery mouth of her old dog Shep close lightly around her ankle. At the same time, she heard the soft voice that had spoken to her moments before. This time she knew without a doubt, the voice was in her mind and it was Old Shep who spoke.

"Gotcha again, Lola."

She said, "Stop that Shep," and patted his gray head. Shep let go and looked up at her for a second. His drool turned cold through her stocking. Then he turned suddenly and scampered off like a young pup. Thinking he wanted to play, she chased after him. He disappeared behind the tree. Lola walked quickly around the trunk, even doubled back once or twice. She stopped with her back to the tree and called his name, but he was nowhere in sight. He had just vanished. His wagging tail held high and his mooning rear end were the last things she saw of Shep.

Her mother waited for her on the porch and said, "I hate to tell you this Lola, but old Shep died this morning."

"But I just saw him beside the oak tree. He snuck up on me, like he always does, and slobbered my ankle." She felt her still-wet stocking as proof to herself of what had happened.

Her mother had cocked her head to one side and squinted her eyes, the way she did when she thought Lola was fibbing.

"I don't know what you saw up there Lola, but I'm

sure it wasn't Shep; unless you uncovered him. That's where your father and I buried him this morning."

Mrs. Bobo realized she had been dreaming when she saw her reflection in the glass of the front door. She shook the memory of her days on the farm from her mind and decided the voice she had just heard was also in her head. She knocked again. This time, she distinctly heard a voice in her mind say, "Please come in, Mrs. B."

Jack said in a loud whisper, "Focus! Will you please stop inviting her in?"

Focus ignored his pleas and waited expectantly opposite the door for Lola's entrance. Jack's movements distracted her. She watched him slide, with his back to the wall and still holding the basketball. He stopped when he reached the corner next to the door.

'Try to relax, Jack; she probably won't even notice the new you.'

He tried to ignore Mrs. B's knocks, hoping she would give up and go home, but she didn't. To Jack's chagrin, Lola let herself in with a key he had given her so she could come in and clean while he was away.

She opened the door just far enough to poke her head in and shout.

"Yoo-hoo, Jack. It's me! Mrs. Bobolinsky!"

Jack dropped the ball, fumbled it, caught it again and tried to tuck it back under his arm just as Lola attempted to open the door all the way. The door struck the ball and shoved it into Jack's stomach knocking the wind out of him.

When the door bounced back, she pushed on it again, then again. Each time the door bounced she heard a "Woof!" sound. Lola wondered what was behind the door that would make such a noise. Jack didn't have a dog, but if he did, its presence sure wasn't bothering Focus. Whatever it was, was big. Being a direct person and caution be damned, she grabbed the door handle and pulled the door away from the wall. She laughed, "Ha?" in a single burst of air. It was more of a question than a laugh.

Her reaction was a calm one, as if seeing Jack standing behind the door in a furry costume holding a basketball in front of his stomach, was an everyday event. Giving him a quizzical look, Lola closed the door as if nothing out of the ordinary were taking place. She then turned to face him, hands on hips, and feet spread.

Not knowing what else to do, Jack stood there and waited, for what, he had no idea. He was apprehensive, embarrassed, and unsure how Lola was going to react. Sheepishly, he said, "Hi, Mrs. Bobo."

In her flat manner of speaking she replied, "Hi yourself. What in the world are you doing behind the door? Are you going to stand there all day? Isn't it the wrong time of the year for Halloween tricks? . . . Oh! I get it, you were trying to scare me, right?

"No!" Jack protested, "I wasn't trying to - - -"

"Well it won't work. I have nerves of steel."

Jack, relieved that Lola was not frightened, watched her remove layer upon layer of warm clothes. She dressed this way the year around. Jack often wondered how she survived the hot Phoenix summers. She justified her winter clothes by saying it was cold for this time of year. The knit hat covering her white hair matched her red wool gloves. She wore a heavy high-collared coat on top of a pullover sweater. All of this she hung on the clothes tree.

Underneath the layers, she wore a long sleeved, mid calf, flower print dress with a white knit collar and cuffs. She had to sit in the chair to peal off her galoshes.

At the end of this tiresome routine, she stood, and from her oversized purse pulled out an apron and tied it around her waist.

All this preparation to thwart the elements, whatever they might be, puzzled Jack; after all, it wasn't as if she had to travel a great distance to arrive at his house. She lived next door. As she adjusted her apron, Jack recalled how this lovable seventy-year-old neighbor had become such an integral part of his life.

Almost two years had passed since Jack took her portrait, and she had agreed to clean his house for one month as payment. Although she had more than paid her debt, she continued to clean, never demanding anything from him. Every so often, Jack tried, to no avail, to make her understand she no longer had to clean the house, but she always had an excuse to hang onto the house key and a reason to continue the cleaning. As far as Jack knew, Lola had no family living in Phoenix. He suspected Lola stayed in his life because she liked to mother him. If she ever did decide to stop coming over, Jack would miss her greatly.

Satisfied her apron was on correctly, she turned from the clothes tree and started for the kitchen, but stopped and turned back to Jack.

"By the way, have I ever thanked you for taking my picture? My kids loved it. Why don't you take off that . . . that, whatever it is costume, then come to the kitchen and I'll fix you a bowl of soup?" She said this as she walked toward the kitchen. Jack followed, trying to explain about his hair.

"I don't want any soup. About this hair--it's real and I . . ."

She turned to face him. "So! You really were trying to scare me, weren't you? If that's what you want, I'll act scared for you."

"No, Mrs. B. I wasn't--you don't have to . . . "

Before Jack could continue, she started to shuffle in a tight circle and flap her arms. She spoke with no emotion or feeling in her voice.

"Help---Oh, help---Murder---My virginity is threatened--Help--save me from the monster." She stopped suddenly; hands on hips again. "How was that Jack?"

"Just fine, Lola."

"If that wasn't good enough, I could run through the house and scream for real!"

Frustrated, Jack shouted at her. "Will you please listen to me! I'm trying to tell you, my hair. . ."

"Well you don't have to shout." She paused, looked offended, then continued, "You know, you could double for the Sun's monkey in that get-up."

"It's a gorilla."

"Gorilla? Monkey? Shmonky? Whatever." With that, she picked up Focus, who had been rubbing against her legs, and marched quick-step into the kitchen. She put the cat on the sink counter, removed two or three plastic containers from the refrigerator, and dumped their contents into a pan.

'Meow, Mrs. B.', thought Focus.

"Meow to you too, Focus. I wondered who was talking in my mind. Do you know how you do it?" Before Focus could answer, Lola went on, "If you don't know, it doesn't matter; it works and that's good enough for me."

'I'm not sure how it works, but I think the ability came to me after eating some fantastic tasting stuff in Jack's photo lab. Jack calls it, "Muck," and thinks it smells bad.'

"Well, there is a strong odor in the house. Incidentally, your hair looks nice."

"Thank you," said Jack.

"I was talking to Focus."

"Well talk to me!" he said forcefully. "I'm trying to make you understand about this hair."

"Jack, don't look so sad. You did your best to scare me and it didn't work. I could work up a good scream, but screaming is bad for the throat you know. My late husband, Wayne--or was that Lane? He died of a bad throat."

'What killed him?' asked Focus.

"They hung him for horse thieve'n. He never did get over it."

She put the pan of soup on the stove to heat and started fixing a pot of coffee.

Jack listened to this mental conversation, but was not yet ready to accept its reality.

"I have to ask you, Lola. Why do you talk to Focus as if she understands what you're saying, and then act as if she is going to answer you?"

"Because she does, and I understand her. She's extremely intelligent, you know."

"You're serious; you really hear each other in your minds."

"Yes!" Mrs. B. and Fo cus answered mentally at the same time.

"Well, if you hear her and I hear her, it must mean the mind talk is real, and I haven't lost my senses-not yet anyway. Okay, Focus, I'll admit it, we have been conversing."

Purring loudly, Focus jumped to the floor and rubbed against Jack's legs.

'I love you Jack.'

"I love you too," said Jack. Focus jumped back up

onto the counter and Mrs. B. whispered to her.

"It looks as though you've been able to penetrate his thick skull."

"What did you say?" asked Jack. "Never mind. I don't want to know. Lola, I need to talk to you about this hair."

She completely ignored his request as she placed a steaming bowl of soup on the table in front of him, then cracked a raw egg into it.

"Eat," she commanded.

"What is this? It smells worse than the house odor."

"Health food. Garlic, egg, and oyster soup. It'll keep you from being peaked."

"I am not peaked!"

She grabbed his face between her hands and with her thumbs pulled his lower eyelids down and looked intently into the whites of his eyes. Jack struggled to remove her hands from his face.

"Peaked!" she exclaimed.

Exasperated, he pushed her hands away, "Will you stop that?"

Mrs. Bobo left the table long enough to pour two steaming cups of coffee and return with them. She sat opposite Jack. "Eat your soup."

"I might be hairy, but I'm not nuts or peaked, and I'm not going to eat this stupid soup. I don't think you understand. This hair is growing all over me."

Jack believed if she could feel his shaggy coat, it would convince her the hair was real. He stretched his left arm out across the table, grasped her left hand, put it on his arm, and held it there.

"Now! Do you see? This is real hair. Go ahead, pull it."

She patted his arm. Then, in a surprise move, she reached across the table, grabbed a hand full of chest hair and nearly pulled him out of his chair.

"Yiiieee! Let go! Damn! Not that hard! That hurt!"

Mrs. B. reacted by yelling and jumping back. At that moment she realized the hair was real. Her eyes wide, she looked at Jack, and then at the black hair between her fingers. She turned pale and backed away from the table.

"I--a--I think my steel nerves just rusted. You're telling me the truth--this is hair. Not a costume?" The reality of her discovery sank in. "This is real hair!"

"That's what I've been trying to tell you," said Jack.

'Big deal, so is mine,' thought Focus.

"Don't be a smart aleck, I can see that Jack has a real problem." Not sure what to do, she leaned against the counter and dusted the hair from her fingers. Then she smoothed her apron with her hands and tried to compose herself.

"I think you can see the problems this hair is causing me. I can't go to work; I can't even go outside! Someone might throw a net over me."

"How in the world did you ever get into this fix in the first place?"

"You remember Jill and Bert?"

"All too well!"

"My problems started when I caught her cheating on me with Bert. I went into a rage and . . . "

She interrupted him. "All that hair reminds me of my fourth husband, Arthur. He had hair all over, but it was curly and felt like steel wool." She smiled at the memory. "He kept me polished, he did. No. Wait. I remember. It wasn't Arthur, it was Amos. Arthur was my agent when I danced in Vaudeville--did you know I was a dancer?"

"No, I . . ."

Lola had interrupted him so many times, Jack was getting used to it.

"I was billed as BOBO and Her Magic Fans. I looked a lot better in the nude than Jill does, and I think I still do." Her eyes glazed over. She had a dreamy look about her as she picked up two plastic place mats from the table.

"I loved to dance with my beautiful white-feather fans." She held the place mats as if they were her fans, one in front, one in back, as a fan dancer would. She changed their positions as she sang.

"St. Louis Women, Ta-Dah-Da-Da-Da-Da." Lola swayed and twirled to a rhythm only she could hear, and for a moment she was transported back on stage at a burlesque house. She reveled in the sounds of clapping hands and whistles from her audience. Their feet stomped to a rhythm supplied by a trumpet, a piano, and a base drum.

Lost in a trance, and remembering those days, she stopped her dance, but held her makeshift fans in place. One in front. One in back.

'That was beautiful, Mrs. B. If I had hands to clap with, I would,' said focus.

"Yes, that was nice Lola, but could we get back to my problem?"

Mrs. Bobo, still lost in her reverie, did not hear Jack.

"Hello! Mrs. B!" Jack's loud voice brought Lola back to the present. She came back startled and disoriented. "What!" she shouted, then put the place-mats back on the table. Now she felt uneasy with Jack and kept her distance.

"Lola. I'm not a danger to you, and I don't think my hair growth is contagious. Unless you happen to go into the darkroom and get some muck on you, you won't grow any hair. Now, come sit with me and drink your coffee."

'He's okay, Lola. Just consider him a big, fuzzy, pussy cat.' Focus patted his arm then began grooming him by licking his hair.

"Stop it, Focus. That's nice of you but it's distracting."

'Sorry, I was just trying to help.'

"I don't know what to do about this hair. As soon as I cut it, it grows right back. Do either of you have any ideas?"

"Tell me how this happened," said Lola. "Maybe the three of us can figure something out. You listen too, Focus,"

'Oh! I will. I want to see if he tells the story the way it really happened.'

Jack absently stroked Focus from her head to her tail.

'I'll give you an hour to stop that,' purred Focus.

"You know, Jack," said Lola, "With all that hair to support, you'll need a lot of iron, Epstein's salts, and a good dose of milk of mag--nolia."

"--nesia," corrected Jack.

"Bless you," said Mrs. B. "Now, tell me what happened?"

Jack had no difficulty recalling every event that led up to this hairy moment, and he tried to tell her what happened without getting angry. It was'nt easy. When he finished his woeful tale, Mrs. Bobolinks pored fresh coffee, then sat opposite him. Focus lay on the table, her front paws tucked under her chest as she watched and listened to her two favorite humans.

"I see your problem, I think!" said Lola, "Focus, do you see his problem?"

'I don't see a problem at all. I think he looks handsome; however, he will have to develop a strong tongue; that's a whole bunch of licking.'

EIGHT

"You're talking to Focus again. At this point, I don't care; I'll take all the help I can get." Focus put a paw on Jack's arm and looked up into his face.

'You're learning, Jack.' He stroked her head then stood and paced the kitchen, brushing the hair out of his eyes as he walked, something he hadn't been able to do in sometime.

Mrs. B. looked concerned for Jack and tried to imagine how frustrating his condition must be to him.

"I read something in the paper recently about a scientist doing research on growing hair, but it looks as if you accidentally found the formula."

"I read that too. The trouble is, I've forgotten what was in most of the containers--let me think--besides a couple of gallons of used film fix and other developing chemicals, there were half eaten peanut butter and banana sandwiches."

'Oh. Yuck! Be still my stomach,' thought Focus.

"You call that food?" chimed in Mrs. B.

"Don't interrupt," said Jack, as he tried to remember more. "There was some moldy orange juice and moldy V-8 juice, a gallon jug of fiberglass resin and its catalyst, plus a lot of stuff in jars that I don't recall at all."

Mrs. B. said. "If you could remember . . . "

"Wait a minute. What are we talking about? I've got to figure out a way to get rid of this hair before it ruins my life!"

Focus had an idea, 'Why don't you ask Fred, your chemist friend to analyze it. That might tell you how to get rid of it?'

"You see, I told you she was smart."

"Analyze it! Of course! That might be the answer!"

Jack called Fred on the kitchen phone.

"Hello, Fred? This is Jack. I know you're about to leave for home, but I need . . ."

"Jack! Where were you today? I've been hearing strange stories all day about you and that powerful odor you had when you came over to my place."

"I'll explain later. Right now, I need a favor. Could you drop by my place on the way home?"

"Sure, if it's important to you."

"It's very important, I can assure you. See you in a few minutes?" He hung up and turned to Mrs. Bobo.

"I'll need a jar or something to put a sample in. Do I have any jars around here, Mrs. B?"

"I have some canning jars at home; I'll go get them."

Fred arrived a few minutes before sundown and parked at the curb in front of Jack's house. Jack watched him arrive from concealment behind the ivy-covered trellis of the front porch. Before Fred started up the steps, Jack spoke to him, hoping not to frighten him.

"Fred, stop right there for a minute. I had an accident in the dark room. It has to do with that odor I had on me when I came to your house.

Now I don't want to frighten you, but I do look different, so come up on the porch; I'm here behind the ivy." Fred stopped on the top step as Jack moved into the light.

Jack's appearance did frighten Fred. He gulped and said loudly, "What the hell is this?"

"Not so loud," cautioned Jack. "You might attract attention." Fred, unsure of the situation, backed up almost falling from the top step. Jack grabbed his arm and pulled him onto the porch.

Fred said, "You think I'll attract attention. What do you think you'll do in that outfit? It looks real!"

"It is real. This isn't a costume. I grew it."

Fred was incredulous. "You what?"

"That's what I said; the stuff that made the stink in the dark room grows hair."

"We should go into the house and talk about this. The smell out here makes my eyes water."

"If you think this is bad, you should have been here yesterday. Your nose will get used to the odor in a few minutes."

"I can't imagine it being worse than this!"

Naturally, Audry and Mavis witnessed Fred's arrival.

"That's Fred Wong. He works with Jack at the college," said Audry.

"Is he French?'

"No, Wong is Chinese."

"Then I guess he won't be staying long."

"Oh, and why not?"

"Well, you know what they say about Chinese food."

"No, I don't."

"Never mind then."

"Look! Someone's on the porch wearing a monkey suit. It sounds like Jack; he just frightened the poop out of Fred."

Jack said, "I know you find it hard to believe, but this darkroom muck really does cause hair to grow."

"Did you have to drink the whole thing?"

"I didn't drink any. I just got a little of it on my hands and it grew hair all over my body. Let's go in."

"Here comes Lola now," said Mavis.

"What's that she's carrying?"

"Looks like a jar--the same kind dad used to get his gin in."

"I'll bet they're going to have a party."

"Must be a costume party."

Moments later, Mrs. Bobo came in carrying a quart size Mason jar with a two part lid and sat it on the table.

"Hi Fred."

"Hi Mrs. B."

"That should get you started," said Lola. "I'm going home. I have plenty of jars, if you need more."

Focus projected. 'Want some company Mrs. B.? I'm tired of the game here.'

"Sure. Come along, we can watch the TV."

The two men watched as she held the door open for the cat then closed it behind her.

Fred seemed a bit bewildered. "Was she talking to us? Or . . ."

"No. To Focus."

"But . . .?"

"Don't ask. You wouldn't believe what I told you."

"Okay, but can you tell me what the jar is for?"

Jack picked the jar up and unscrewed the lid. "It has to do with the favor I'm asking of you."

Fred said, "I'm not too sure I want to hear about this."

"I'm going to put some hair-muck in the jar and seal it with the lid. I'd like you to take it to your lab at the college and analyze it; find out what's in it that causes hair to grow. I'll help, if I can. Will you do it?"

Fred pondered Jack's request for about a second, then decided even an idiot could see the potential importance of a find like this.

"I can try, but I'm not sure I have the right equipment to break it down."

Jack took a table knife from one drawer and a pair of rubber gloves from another.

"The stuff is thick--like taffy candy. I think I can cut it with the knife if I do it quickly. Here, you hold the lid and let's go see if I'm right."

He was right and after a few tries he managed to whack off small golf-ball size chunks and flip them into the jar until he filled the jar. He turned the two-part lid on until it was tight, then put the muck filled jar into a plastic bag.

"Old friend, your findings might make you famous. It's a hairy job but you're just the man who can do it."

"I'm not so sure about that, but 'we' won't know until 'we' try. Everyone should be gone from the chemistry building by now; I'll go on over and get started."

Before Jack handed over the jar, he said, "Be sure you wear rubber gloves. If you get this muck on your hands you could end up looking like me. One more thing, whatever you do, don't tell anyone what this stuff is; I mean, nobody!"

He handed Fred the prize. "I'll handle it as if it were a jar of nitroglycerin."

"When it's darker outside, I'll join you at the lab." Fred tucked the package under his arm and held onto it with the other.

When he climbed into his car, he stuffed the jar in the crack between the seats to keep it from rolling around, let out a sigh relief and drove the car toward the college lab.

Fred was hunched over a microscope, his eye to the eyepiece as he adjusted the focus on another glass slide. He looked away long enough to make a notation on a yellow legal pad. A knock at the door didn't break his concentration. He called out, "Come!"

Jack opened the door, stepped into the room and looked furtively back down the hall before he closed the door. Fred looked to see what Jack was doing. He did a double-take and laughed at the comic figure that was Jack. He had on a long trench coat with the collar turned up, dark glasses, and a Humphry Bogart hat. Fred wished he had a camera.

"You look like a foreign spy in that getup."

"Well, if anyone did see me, they couldn't see how hairy I am. I covered as running from the police because someone reported seeing a chimp on the loose. Have you had any luck identifying the ingredients?"

"So far, only those elements we already know about."

Jack handed him a list of the things he could remember that were in the refrigerator.

Jack noticed Fred's new image."I told you to be careful handling this stuff. It's obvious what you've been doing."

"I tried to be careful." He had a clump of black hair growing out of one ear, and the hair growing from his nose and upper lip looked like a Fu Manchu mustache."

Fred looked at the list. It wasn't much help.

"A peanut - butter and banana sandwich?"

"I was out of onions."

After three hours of steady effort, Jack was leaned back in a chair, his feet crossed on a desk. The yellow legal pad on his lap was for taking notes dictated by Fred as he finished each test. Fred pushed his chair back, stood, stretched, and yawned.

"Look Jack, we're getting nowhere and I have classes in the morning. What say we stop for the night and try again tomorrow?"

Jack dropped his feet to the floor. "You're right, I'm bushed. Thanks for trying. I'll see you tomorrow." Jack put on his spy outfit and left. Fred leaned against the work table, his back to the open jar of muck, his mind still on the analysis. A big tom cat, named Duke, suddenly appeared in the open window. He looked at Fred, then at the jar, a scant three feet away.

Duke wondered, 'Could that be it?' He leaped silently to the table, crept stealthily forward, savored the grand aroma as the exotic fumes assaulted his senses, 'This must be it!' then without hesitation he buried his nose in the jug of muck.

Fred's concentration was disrupted when he heard a slurping, eating noise and loud purring coming from behind him. He turned around and came face to face with Duke's bright-yellow eyes. Duke licked his lips, savoring the flavor while he watched Fred closely.

'It took me hours to track this down. It's Fantastic!

Don't move a muscle hair-ball, this is all mine.'

Duke wanted more, but before he had a chance to go for it, Fred hit him with the yellow pad and shouted.

"Scat! Get out of here!"

Duke yowled and dove out through the open window

"And don't come back!"

Fred slid the window closed, turned the lid back on the jar, then held it up to the light.

"Cat, I don't know how much of this you ate, but I'm willing to bet it was worth a lot of money."

Duke did not give up easily. He jumped back to the ledge and tried to hook a claw to the side of the metal sliding window to open it, but it was too tight. He watched Fred open the lab refrigerator and place the jar inside.

'I don't know what that wonderful tasting stuff is, but it has done something to my brain. I have a new awareness.'

Fred put on his sweater, turned out the lights and left. Duke jumped to the ground and sat licking his lips and twitching his nose.

'I can still smell that exotic odor. Hey, it's coming from that guy in the hat and trench coat.' Duke stayed in the shadows and followed Jack to his car and watched him drive away. Duke gave chase. 'You might be faster than me mister, but wherever you go, I'll track you down, I will find you,' thought Duke.

The cat had no trouble following the scent left in the air by the departing car and decided to take his time in its pursuit.

Back at the college lab, Fred had returned and went straight to the phone. He called Gray Pharmaceutical Company where Dr. Don Swaite, an old college friend, worked.

.Dr. Swaite was thirty, overweight, short, balding and had an attitude problem. He was a research assistant and achieved that position by back-stabbing anyone who blocked his climb up the corporate ladder. The management loved him.

"I don't know why I didn't think of him sooner--it's only ten thirty and I know he likes to work late . . . Hello, Dr. Don Swaite please."

"This is Don. Who's this."

"Hey Don, it's Fred Wong."

"Who?"

"What do you mean, who? We roomed together in college for three years and you say, who!"

"Yeah! What do you want Fred? I'm very busy and don't have time for reminiscing."

"You know Don, I'd forgotten what a disagreeable jack- ass you are."

Don laughed, "That's me."

"What I want, is to find out if you know anything about hair-growth chemicals and what the market might be for something like that." There was a silent pause, then all Fred could hear on the line was heavy breathing.

"Don? Are you there?"

Don oozed with friendliness when he spoke.

"Fred, have you come up with something that grows hair?"

Fred decided to hold off a little. He could tell by Don's voice that he was holding his breath, waiting for an answer. At the same time, by calling Don, Fred was breaking his promise to Jack not to reveal what the muck was. Now he found himself in a fix.

"I don't have anything, but a friend of mine was working on a formula that showed some promise and I told him I would look into it for him. I have a sample, and Don, this is extremely confidential, but I feel I can trust you not to talk to anyone about this. Can I trust you, Don?"

Fred detected an unnatural eagerness, even restrained laughter in Don's voice, but in seeming sincerity Don said, "Well of course you can trust me, Fred. Where are you calling from?"

"I'm at the college lab. Do you think you could break down the ingredients if I gave you a sample?"

"Why do you need a breakdown?" asked Don.

"Because we have no idea what's in it. There is no formula, and I don't have the necessary equipment at the lab to analyze it properly."

"Bring me a sample in the morning and I'll take a look-see. I won't promise anything though until I've had a chance to study it thoroughly."

"How much do you think it will cost?"

Dr. Swaite, Mr. super-friendly, answered, "Hey, since we're old friends, it won't cost you a dime. After all, what are friends for!"

"That's terrific. I'll drop off a sample first thing in the morning."

After they hung up, the expression on Dr. Don Swaite's face was positively wicked. He even chuckled, then shouted.

"Morning! Like hell! I know a gold-mine when I hear one!"

Don grabbed his coat and slipped it on as he dashed to the elevator. It let him off at the basement parking level.

A few minutes later, his headlights out, he coasted to a stop down the street from the college and waited. He could see the lab lights were still on. Soon they went out. Don waited until he was sure Fred was out of the area, then walked the half-block to the lab building. He found the window the cat escaped through unlocked, slid it open, and with great, but determined effort, hefted his rotund bulk inside, and closed the window.

He found the jar of muck, put it in a bag, and left unnoticed through the front door of the building. Back in his car, he sat for a couple of minutes getting his breath back. He almost fainted from the exertion and excitement, but was generally pleased with his success; he had on a wicked Jack Nicholson grin.

"That was easy and dangerously fun." Slipping the jar from his coat pocket, he hefted it. "Whatever this stuff is, it's extremely heavy and there's a terrible odor coming from it. I'll start work on this tonight."

* * *

Duke arrived at Jack's house and recognized the car he had been chasing parked in the driveway.

'I told you I would find you--you must have a bunch of that stuff stashed close by; the odor is powerful and it's making me hungry. I smell something else coming from that house next door. I think I'll check it out.' Duke jumped the fence into the yard and sniffed around a garbage can.

'Ummm. Something smells mighty fine.'

He knocked the can over and the lid clattered to the ground. As he climbed inside the can to claim his reward, Mrs. B. came out to see what all the noise was about. She could see a cat's tail sticking out of the can, reached for her trusty broom and whacked the can with it. Duke screeched, jumped straight up and smacked his head a good one. Slightly dazed, he scampered out of the can and zigzagged toward the fence.

"If you're that hungry, why don't you come in and

have something fresh?" She started to close the door, not realizing the cat understood her, until the cat stopped and took a few tentative steps toward her. She waited to see what he was going to do. To her surprise the cat spoke to her in her mind.

'Were you just talking to me lady?'

"Sure was."

'I am kinda hungry. I had a snack earlier at the college of some great stuff, but it only made me hungry for more.'

"I think I know what you got into. What would you like to eat?"

'A five pound tuna would be nice.'

"Sorry, I'm fresh out. Come in and I'll see what I can stir up for you." She held the door open and Duke strolled into her kitchen, sat in the middle of the floor and checked out the room.

'Best equipped kitchen I've ever seen. It's also the first time I've ever been in one.'

"How long have you been talking to people?"

'You're my first. Is it me, or is it you that makes our talking possible?'

"I think it's a combination of that stuff you ate and my ability to hear what you think. You can stay with me, if you want to. I'll keep you well fed, and I could use the company. Also, there is someone I want you to meet."

'Sounds good to me. There is one thing though; I've slept on roof tops, under porches and a hundred other places, but never in a house. Can I sleep inside?'

"Whenever you want."

NINE

Fred stood in front of the cold-box, the door open. He checked each shelf, in front of and behind every item, but could not find the sample of hair-stuff.

"I know I'm forgetful, but I'm almost positive I put that jar in here. I should call Don and tell him I don't have it."

Don answered after one ring. "Listen, ahh, Don, I can't find the sample I was going to bring you. I'll have to get another one."

It took great restraint for Don not to laugh when Fred called. The look on his face was one of devilish delight as he studied the jar before him. What he saw was not a jar full of gooey muck, but a jar full of gold colored dollar signs. His inner excitement made him feel as if he had just won a national lottery. He stroked the side of the jar with a rubber gloved hand.

Then Don continued with his deception, "Damn it Fred. You're wasting my time. Are you sure you ever had any of this stuff?"

"Don't be such a jerk--of course I had it. I'll call you tomorrow after I have another sample." He hung up with his finger and dialed Jack's number.

"Jack's not going to like this." Jack answered on the second ring.

"Hi, Jack. Say, I've misplaced the jar of muck somewhere in the lab; Could I come over and get another."

"What do you mean, misplaced? The least you could do is guard the jar with your life.

"Oh, I'll find it. Don't worry. You know how cluttered it gets in the lab. I probably covered it with something."

"Okay. Come on over," said Jack.

Mrs. Bobo was in the kitchen with Jack. She had just placed a box of quart Mason jars on the table.

"Is this going to be enough?"

"I hope so. Thanks again."

$$* \quad * \quad *$$

In the darkroom, Jack had filled eight jars with the concentrated muck and lined them up on the table. When a knock came at the front door, he assumed it was Fred so he hurriedly screwed the last lid on and walked quickly to the door. Through the door window, he could see it wasn't Fred, but Jill and Bert and he angrily yanked the door open.

"What the hell do you two want?"

Jill was startled by the hairy thing that held the door open. She stepped back and planted her spiked high-heel on the top of Bert's foot. Bert went into a circling impression of an Indian rain-dance and accompanied himself with a chant; "Oh!-that-hurts." "Oh!-that-hurts."

Jill spoke harshly. "It's not funny, whoever you are. Can't you see he's in pain?"

Jack laughed again. "Yes, I can, and I love it!"

"You're a sadist!"

"Thank you very much."

"We're here to see Jack Stump. Would you please call him to the door?"

"He's not here. Who are you people anyway? What the hell do you want?"

Jill was not to be put off easily. She caught a certain tone, an inflection from the creature before her.

"Jack? Is that you? What are you doing in that silly monkey suit?"

"Yeah, it's me, but it's not a costume. Now, why are you here?"

"May we come in?"

"Why?"

"We need to talk to you."

"Oh, I guess so. As long as you don't stay long."

Jack ushered them into the living room. Jill and Bert sat on the couch. Jack stood by the fire place and waited for them to explain their presence. Jack could see they were ill-at-ease and he would do everything possible to make them more so. He said irritably, "Well? Why are you here?"

Bert spoke first. "Just out of curiosity, why are you wearing that costume?"

"The odor is still in the house, as you can tell. It's coming from some chemicals that accidentally got mixed in the darkroom. I got some on me and it caused hair to grow all over my body--surprise! The hair is real!"

"You can't be serious," responded Jill.

A devious plot entered Jack's mind and he tried to act sincere. "I'm very serious. So serious, I'm forming a company to manufacture; 'Jack's Hair Growth Products".

He emphasized each word as he spoke. "I don't have all the details worked out yet; but I can predict, if you invest in this company now, you'll both make millions!"

Jill and Bert were caught up in Jack's enthusiasm.

"That really sounds exciting, and you would let bygones be bygones and allow us in on the ground floor?" said Bert.

"Sure I would," Jack said with mock sincerity. "After all, we were close friends."

Jill looked at Bert and asked. "What do you think?"

"Well, on the surface it sounds very good, and it's obvious your hair growth stuff works. It looks like a winner to me! When do you plan . . . ?" Bert stopped and waved his hand back and forth at Jill. "Wait! Hold on a minute. Jill! Have you forgotten why we're here?"

"No! I haven't, but his idea sounds good. You said so yourself. I have some money saved and Jack's plan seems like a good . . ."

Bert stopped her again with a wave of his hand. "No! No! You don't understand; now listen to me," he scolded. Jill folded her arms, pouted and glared at Burt, then leaned back on the couch.

Jack smiled and chuckled. "Don't fight kiddies."

"You listen too, Jack. Besides coming here to pick up our things, we wanted to let you know that I'm representing Jill in a palimony suit."

"In a what?" Jack, his fists clinched at his sides, took a step toward Bert. Bert pushed himself back into the couch padding, but stayed his ground," A palimony suit, and another thing, since you brought it up, Jill won't have to invest in anything. She will be entitled to a sizable percentage of any proceeds realized from the sale of this--ahh--hair growth stuff."

Jill was now all for Bert and took hold of his hand. "That's right Jack! What are you trying to pull? Were you trying to cheat me out of-a-something?" She looked shocked.

Jack bent into a crouch, as if he were about to leap. His fists still knotted, he said, "I'll give you something real to sue me for, if you don't get your greedy butts out of my house."

He raised his fists, lunged at them and growled threateningly. They raced for the front door. Bert got there first and opened it, but Jill shoved him aside and sprinted past. Bert was close behind. He turned back to see if Jack was still after him; he was, and Bert stepped quickly onto the porch and closed the door in Jack's face.

Fred had arrived and approached the porch steps just as Jill ran past him. She looked frightened.

"Jill! What happened?"

From the sidewalk, she stopped long enough to say excitedly, "Don't go in there! Jack is crazy. He has completely lost his mind!"

From the top step Fred wondered what had happened and watched Jill run to Bert's car and jump in. Fred turned to knock on the door just as Bert came out. Bert turned quickly to get away from the attacking beast and rammed into Fred knocking him down the steps. Fred, unhurt but surprised, got up, dusted himself off, and said, "What the devil was that for?"

Bert said, "Sorry, Fred," but didn't stop to explain as he ran to his Porsche and piled in to join Jill. Seconds later his car weaved off down the street at full speed.

Fred watched these strange antics without a clue to their cause. He scratched his head, shrugged his shoulders, climbed the steps, and knocked on the door. Jack threw the door open, jumped out growling at the unsuspecting Fred, and knocked him sprawling on his back. Jack quickly straddled Fred's skinny frame and grabbed him by the throat. A split second later he recognized his mistake.

"Hi! Fred. Sorry about this, I thought you were that sorry excuse for a lawyer, Bert, coming back."

Fred shouted at Jack, "Get your hands off my throat." Then through tight lips, he said, "My nerves can't take any more of your surprises. Now, if you don't mind," he shouted again, "get-your hairy-ass off me!" Jack got up and helped Fred to his feet.

"I'll make it up to you--come in and I'll buy you a beer."

"The way things are going, you're going to owe me a full keg."

A few minutes later the two old friends sat at the kitchen table drinking a beer.

Fred said, "I need another sample because I couldn't find the sample we had in the lab. I searched everywhere. It's as if it vanished."

"I suppose one jar, more or less, won't make much difference."

Before Fred told Jack about Dr. Don Swaite, he left the table and stood by the sink. He wanted to be out of Jack's reach.

"I have something else to tell you and I want you to control your temper until I've finished--okay?"

"Okay, I guess. What is it?" he asked suspiciously.

"The reason I need another sample, is . . ." He paused, then continued, "A chemist friend of mine, Dr. Don Swaite, who works for a big research outfit, said he could use his companies equipment to analyze the hair-muck, and he wouldn't charge us a cent. Isn't that great?" Fred could see the explosion coming.

Jack's voice started slow and low then built to a violent pitch. "Well damn your hide! I asked you not to tell anyone, and you betray me by telling a friend, someone I don't even know!" Jack was on his feet and pacing the kitchen as he shouted. Fred made sure to keep the table between them.

"Now calm down and listen to me. 'We' don't have a thing until 'we' find out what's in this muck that makes it grow hair." Jack tried to calm himself and sat at the table, still glaring at Fred.

"What do you know about this guy, this Dr. Don Swaite?" Fred felt he was safe now, and joined Jack at the table.

"We were roommates in college. He's a real jerk to know, but a very sharp chemist and I think we can trust him."

"Well, okay, I'll trust your judgment, but for your sake, I hope you're right." Jack was silent for a moment then said, "What I would like to do, is bag up all the jars and take them to the college lab and stash them there. I need to get them out of the house so I can finish cleaning the darkroom. I have some film to develop."

*　　*　　*

When Dr. Swaite opened the stolen sample jar, he closed it quickly. The fumes he released almost knocked him flat. Before he opened it again, he put on an air filter capable of mustard-gas protection. Then, with rubber-gloved hands, he removed the lid long enough to take out a sample on the end of a glass rod. From this he took a pin-head-sized sample and spoke into a tape-recorder microphone.

162

"First step. I have placed a pin-head-sized sample from the concentrate onto a glass slide and will studied it under the microscope."

Don studied the slide for a few minutes, and came to no conclusion. He recognized a few common elements, but the rest of the particles remained a mystery. He tried another approach. "I have placed a live pigskin shaving in a petri dish and applied a pin-head-sized concentrate sample in the center of it."

Before he could cover the dish, the skin quickly absorbed the sample. In seconds inch-high black hair covered the skin patch. Don described this action to the recorder. Also recorded was his reaction.

"Wow! Whatever this shit is, it's potent stuff!"

The doctor tried several other tests, but still could not identify certain parts of the concentrate. He recorded, "So far, some components in this mess defy identification."

He tried another direction by blending it with Gray's standard skin cream. Several tests later, he recorded: "This is batch number ten combined with the last nine mixes making a total of ten gallons. Evidently enough concentrate is still present from the first drop to be effective. Although the growth rate has slowed considerably, it still grows hair on the petri skin sample. I am now going to apply a small amount to my head."

He noted the time and date and removed his gloves and air filter.

Don hesitantly touched the tip of his index finger to the surface of the cream, put it to his scalp and massaged it in. A few seconds later he felt a tingling sensation as his skin reacted. He went to the mirror on the wall and watched dark peach fuzz turn to a full head of black hair. It had been so long since he had hair to groom, he no longer carried a comb. He brushed his new grown hair with a finger-nail bristle brush. It worked fine.

Don was in awe and looked at himself for quite awhile. He was ecstatic. "Hot damn!" he shouted. "I think I've got it!" He did a little jig and laughed with glee. "I can hardly wait to see the faces of those hot shots in R and D when I show them this!"

The palms of Don's hands felt odd and he turned them up to the light. Short black fuzzy hair had grown there. He laughed.

"Well I'll be damned--it's really true!"

TEN

While Mrs. B. unloaded Jack's dishwasher, the kitchen wall phone rang. She answered it, unaware that Jack had come into the kitchen and was standing behind her.

"Stump house. Yes, he's here. Hold on a minute." She put her hand over the mouth piece and called out, "Jack! Telephone!"

"You don't have to shout. I'm right here. Who is it?"

"Ahhhhh!" she shouted and jumped. "Are you trying to give me a stroke? I don't know who it is. Here!" She shoved the receiver into his chest. "Find out for yourself."

'He did that on purpose,' said Focus.

"I know he did. The dirty rat." She gave Jack a mean look. Jack smiled innocently as he talked to the caller.

"Hello--speaking--yes, Mrs. Argile--he's in town!--When?--thanks for calling." He hung up slowly.

In an agonized voice, he said, "Oh! No! Oh, damn! I'm ruined if he comes by. He can't do that. I have to figure out a way to stop him." Jack slumped into a chair, elbows on the table, his head cradled in his hands. He looked miserable.

'He must have a serious problem,' said Focus.

Mrs. Bobo agreed with her. "Problem, Jack?"

"That was Editor Smith's secretary from Autumn Life magazine. He's in town and plans to drop by. If he sees me like this I'll lose the photo assignment for sure. I've got to find a way to get rid of this damn hair." Jack paced around the table. Focus trotted with him.

'Is this a game?'

"No, it's not. I'm really worried. Now listen to me, both of you. If a man comes to the door asking for me and he looks like he might be an editor, tell him I was suddenly called out of town. No wait! That will kill the job too. I have it. Tell him I'm out preparing for the assignment, or tell him I'm sick, I think I am sick."

Jack sat at the table again and put his head down on his crossed arms.

'Sorry, Jack, but I don't know how to lie and I don't think Lola does either. Do you Lola?' said Focus.

Mrs. Bobo came to the table opposite him and leaned her hands on the back of a chair. "I have never knowingly told a lie and I'm not about to start now. Face up to the problem, Jack," Lola went back to the sink and acted busy.

"But if Smith sees me with all this hair, the start of my would-be career is over."

Focus jumped onto the table and sat in front of Jack. He stroked her.

'You don't know that for sure; he might like you better this way. Personally, I think you're much more attractive.' She patted his arm with her paw.

Jack said, "We might have to find that out, and just hope he's a compassionate man."

When Dr. Swaite presented 'his' findings and a jar

of 'his' cream mix to his associates in Gray's new products division, they laughed in his face and threatened to throw him off the roof. Knowing how ambitious he was, and that he couldn't be trusted, they covered their work notes every second he was in their presence.

Don pointed out his new hair. "If you want proof, how do you think I got this hair?"

"That's nothing but a good toupee," they said.

"No! You're all wrong! It's real! If you don't believe me, feel it!" he said desperately.
They almost scalped him trying to pull it off, but were finally convinced it was real and agreed to run a few tests. They assumed Don had invented the formula and asked him for a list of the ingredients; he told them to go to hell.

Unknown to the boys in the R&D lab, Dr. Don Swaite was a nervous wreck. After two days they called him.

"Don, this is Ray in new products, we cut your cream mix three more times and we've made a test application."

Don's nasty side surfaced. "Cut the bull, Ray. What did you find out?"

"Calm down, Don. Try to be civil for a change. We're trying to help you with this."

"Kiss my patootie, Ray," Don knew they were hooked.

"All right, be a jerk if you want to, but do you remember my intern, George, skin-head George?"

"No I don't! Damn it Ray, will you get on with it?"

"Okay! Okay! Just hold on. You might recall a hair cream commercial slogan; 'A little dab'll do ya?' Well, that's all we used on George and today he has a crew-cut.

It's a winner, Don. And in spite of your bad attitude and lack of team spirit, we're excited about the cream's potential. We think it's the biggest breakthrough since the invention of peanut-butter!"

Don was dumb struck. He was sure the cream would get a good response, but not this good; this was great! He could see clearly the money potential from this hair-growth muck would run into the millions.

"Don? . . . Don! Are you still there?"

"Yeah! Ray," he tried to sound casual. "It sounds terrific, Ray."

"How soon will you be ready to go with this?"

"I'll have some figures for you in a couple of days," Don lied.

Don was in a mental and physical sweat. He hadn't been able to identify all the ingredients that made up the formula.

He began to form a scheme. "I must find out where Fred's friend lives, find out how much of this stuff he has--I might even consider offering him a deal, but then--why would I do that if I can get hold of it for nothing. Screw him, he won't even know what happened."

*   *   *

Jack hoped that by cutting his hair close enough, editor Smith might think he was just a hairy kind of guy.

As he stood in the bath tub, he worked the electric hair clippers around his shoulders, neck and head. Hair two inches thick covered the bottom of the tub. Focus sat on the toilet seat watching the futile effort.

'Why bother, Jack, it will just grow back.'

"I have to keep trying. You know Focus, it might only be my imagination, but it seems as though each time I cut it, it grows back slower. I wonder what that means?"

Right after he stepped out of the tub and unplugged the clippers, someone knocked on the front door.

"Quiet Focus, go see who it is."

'I'm not making any noise. Go see for yourself. I can't open doors.'

Following another knock, Jack crawled to the door and peeked out at the corner of the drape. There was a man dressed in a gray pin-stripped suit, a hat and a red tie. "This has to be editor Smith. I'm doomed." The man knocked again. Thinking fast, Jack answered in a weak, raspy voice.

"Who is it?"

"I'm Mr. Smith--from Autumn Life magazine--my secretary called you I believe?"

Jack coughed a couple of times and in the same weak voice he croaked.

"I'm sorry Mr. Smith, but I have a bad case of strep throat," He coughed again, then continued in the same raspy voice. "It's very contagious. Could you call me in a couple of days?" Jack saw the editor step back from the door, take out his handkerchief and hold it over his nose and mouth. The editor was obviously a man concerned about catching other people's germs.

"Sorry to find you under the weather." The editors voice was so muffled, Jack had a hard time understanding him. "I hope you're over this in time to cover your assignment."

"I see the doctor today."

"Fine! I'll check with you in a week." He turned abruptly and scurried off the porch to a waiting cab.

As the cab pulled away, Jack shouted and pounded on the wall. "I-have-got-to-get-rid-of-this-hair!"

'But Jack, it's soooo attractive. Incidentally, I'll give

you a four star meow for that performance. You had me convinced.'

      *   *   *

Don had never been in Chairman Of The Board Gray's offices before. When Don was summoned, he hoped the rumors about the Chairman being the worst tyrant in town were untrue. After a few minutes of sitting on the uncomfortably hard seat, Don was sure the chair had been designed by Space Aliens and only they would fit the chair. He sat as straight backed as he could for a man as rotund as he. It seemed as if he had been waiting for over an hour, when actually, he had only been there a few minutes.

Don leafed through a magazine, but was so nervous and intimidated by being there, he didn't notice the magazine was upside down, nor did anything on the pages he flipped through register on his mind. His right knee started jerking up and down and he had to press on it with both his hands before it stopped bouncing.

Twenty feet across the room, Ms. Doxie, Gray's secretary had lifted her phone to her ear, listened for a second, then put it down.

"You may go in now, Dr. Swaite."

Don heard her speak, but was so nervous, he didn't understand her and she prompted him again.

"Dr. Swaite? You may go in now. Chairman Gray is waiting." Don jumped to his feet as if he had been jabbed with a cattle prod. The magazine fell to the floor, making more noise than a magazine had a right to make.

In his haste, he stepped on the magazine, slipped, caught himself then launched his body toward the huge, imposing double doors. He suddenly pulled up short of his goal, as if he had hit an invisible wall. He reached for the door handle, but his hand shook, and try as he might, he could not touch the handle.   Ms. Doxie gave him a quizzical look.

"Dr. Swaite . . .?"

Don jerked his hand away from the handle and turned toward her.

He stammered.   "Yes? What? Oh good.   He's changed his mind and doesn't want to see me after all. I'll leave quietly."   He headed for the outer door, but Ms. Doxie called to him.

"Wait! Swaite!"

He froze in his tracks. Ms. Doxie continued in a commanding voice, "Mr. Gray is expecting you, and you had better calm your nervous butt and get in there before he calls you again. Now, get over there, open the door, and step inside."

He did as he was told and stepped into hell. Once inside with the door closed behind him, he faced an enormous board-room table. At the other end of the table, in the distance, sat a group of men. He took one step forward and they seemed even further away; then the table turned into the pitching deck of an aircraft carrier and jets were taking off into his face. He shook his head and everything returned to normal.

There were three men on each side of the table. Although they were different in subtle ways, they were clones of Mr. Gray. Each clone wore a light blue blazer and black rimmed glasses. Each had a light covering of peach fuzz on his head and had a big Cuban cigar clamped in the corner of his mouth. They all stared at Don with poker faces. Finally, Chairman Gray spoke.

"Come in Don, I can call you Don, can't I? Good! Come sit here next to me."

When Don looked at the chair, he was positive it

was an electric-chair, but seated, he realized it was ordinary. Gray was smiling and very friendly. Don began to relax a little.

"Don, I called this informal meeting so the boys and I could meet the genius behind the hair-growth cream." Don started to say something but Gray cut him off. "Don't interrupt, boy." The clones all frowned at Don.

Gray smiled around his cigar and smoothed the top of his head.

"I put your hair-growing cream on my chrome-dome this morning and the fuzz has started already." The clones smoothed their fuzzy heads in unison. Don sat stiffly at attention. He was petrified.

"When you're ready to start production, I want you to call me personally. Personally!--do you understand?"

"Yes sir! Call you perso . . ."

"Don't interrupt me, boy. The company--ME! -- will launch the biggest multimedia ad campaign ever attempted with a money-back guarantee and the product will have my name on it. Gray's Hair Growth Cream."

Don was sweating heavily now as Gray leaned close to him. They were almost nose to nose. Cigar smoke engulfed their faces and although Gray had a demonic look about him, he spoke softly, but firmly.

"Now, you listen real close--Dr. Swaite, I'm putting everything on the line for this hair growth cream, and I'm ready to roll. I want to hear from you . . . soon!"

Don almost jumped out of his skin when Gray said-- soon! And again when all the clones leaned toward him, and said, "Soon!" in unison. After that shock, Chairman Gray dismissed him like a school boy and told him to get back to work. Don's legs wouldn't carry him fast enough to get out of the board room.

Back in his lab, Don was still in a sweat and paced the room, talked to himself, waved his arms in the air. Finally, he decided his only chance for success, was to follow Fred until he led the way to the stash of hair-growth concentrate.

ELEVEN

As planned, Jack and Fred loaded the remaining seven jars of muck concentrate into two separate boxes and carried them out to Fred's car, got in and drove off. Almost a block away, and up the street from Jack's house, a large black limousine parked in the shade of a tree. It appeared unoccupied, but when Fred's car pulled away, the good Dr. Don Swaite popped his head up and watched until the departing car turned the corner. It hadn't occurred to Don they might take the jars someplace else. As far as he knew, the jars of concentrate were still somewhere in that house.

The scheming scientist-turned-thief, moved the limo to a spot directly across the street from Jack's house; the house where two of the neighborhood's most informed ladies lived.

Mavis watched Don park.

"Audrey. Who do we know that drives a big-long-black car?"

"No one I can think of. Why?" Audrey looked up from her knitting.

"One just parked out front."

After checking the street and sidewalks in all directions, he saw no one. Before moving into action, Don watched Jack's house for a couple of minutes; making sure he would not be seen. Prior to leaving the limo, he took a credit card from his wallet, and stuck it in his shirt pocket, then squirmed out. He left the door ajar; just in case a hasty retreat was necessary. Furtively he looked up and down the street as he hustled from the limo to Jack's front door. With his credit card, he quickly opened it, and stepped inside.

Mavis said, "Did you see that? The chubby man that drove the big expensive car just let himself into Jack's house. He must be a close friend."

"Might be someone important," said Audrey.

Before Don closed the door, he stuck his head out, and looked the neighborhood over again. When he determined no one had seen him, he closed the door and boldly called out.

"Hello! Is anyone home?"

If someone had been home, he had a lame excuse for being in the house. He would pose as an environmental government agent sent to investigate the possession of illegal chemicals. His other plan was to run like hell.

Don mistakenly believed he hadn't been seen entering the house. Not only had Mavis and Audrey watched him enter, but so had a curious cat sitting on the porch rail.

'That man just broke into my house! I better get Mrs. Bobo, and fast..'

"Look at Focus run!" said Mavis. "That man must have frightened her."

Focus dashed next door to Lola's back-screen-door and anchored herself, spread-eagle. Her claws set onto the screen, she repeatedly called: 'Lola! Help. Mrs. B! Mrs. B!'

Lola was there in a second and opened the door. "You don't have to tear the door off. I heard you calling." She picked Focus up. "You're all fuzzed out. What's the matter dear, is that cocker-spaniel after you again?"

'No! It's much worse than that. A man-a burglar-just broke into my house!'

"You mean Jack's house?" She sat at the table and put Focus in front of her.

'Well, I like to think of it as my house. I let Jack live there with me. Anyhow, what are we going to do about that burglar? He's in there, throwing things around and stealing everything. I'm sure of it.'

"We'll just see about that! I just got the place cleaned."

Another voice joined in the conversation. Duke, doing his John Wayne impression, lay on the seat of the other chair and sat up. His head appeared over the edge of the table.

'I could go over there and show him what a Mutant Ninja cat can do to his face.'

'Who's that talking?' said Focus. Then she saw Duke. She spit at him, arched her back, and her hair stood on end.

Duke stayed calm, and in his best Bogart accent addressed her.

'Cool it sweetheart, that act won't work with me-- You wana make some babies, beautiful? I think I'm in love, Mrs. B. Who's the doll?'

"Focus, meet Duke, he lives here with me. Duke, meet Focus, she lives next door with Jack Stump." Duke hopped up on the table and rubbed noses with Focus.

'Is he the guy with all the hair and smells like a million bucks? Does he have any more of that fantastic elixir of life?'

'Yes, Jack has several jars of the stuff, but he keeps it locked up and won't let me near it.' Focus paused, then continued. 'I just realized, Duke is mind-talking with us. It seemed so natural, I didn't even notice.' They rubbed noses again and Focus surprised Duke by doing her impression of May West. 'I'll talk to you later, big boy.'

"We had better do something about that burglar, and quick!" said Mrs. B.

'Call the cops,' said Focus'

"I don't think so," said Lola. "They weren't exactly friendly the last time they were here. We will have to handle this ourselves."

Don dashed from room to room; frantic in his quest. There was only one room locked. He found a pass key in a bowl on the hall table, right where Jack left it and opened the darkroom door.

"This has to be where it is. I know that smell." He went through everything in the lab and found nothing.

"Audrey! Look!"

"What is it now? You made me lose a stitch."

"Here comes Lola followed by two cats and Lola's carrying her broom like it was a rifle. She looks very determined. What do you suppose she's going to do?"

Don, meanwhile, was having no luck. "Damn! They must have taken it all with them. I should get the hell out of here before they come back."

Hurrying to the front door, he opened it, ready to dash for the limo; instead, he stopped in the doorway. Startled, and slightly frightened, Don backed up. Confronting him was an elderly woman holding a broom. Two cats sat on each side of her and the three of them blocked his way. Mrs. B. held her broom at the ready.

Instead of revealing his fright, Don turned aggressive and demanded. "Who are you?"

Calmly, Lola said, "The question is, Buster, who are you and what are you doing in this house?" Don tried to bluff her.

"Lady, I don't have time for this and what I'm doing here is none of your business. Now move out of my way!" Mrs. Bobo didn't budge.

"Hold it right there, Buckaroo. The cops will be here any second. What did you steal?"

Don took a step toward her and in a hostile voice, said, "I don't want to hurt you lady, but I will if you don't get out of my face!" He tried to get around her and she poked him in the stomach with the broom handle. He doubled over and she smacked him on the head with the broom. Gasping for air, he held his stomach with one hand and tried to protect his head with the other.

'That should hold him for awhile. What do we do now?' said Focus.

Duke, as John Wayne, added. 'Mister, you're messing with the Ninja Housekeeper now. You might as well give up.'

"Duke! Focus! If this bushwhacker moves again, eat him alive!"

Don, still trying to get his breath back, couldn believe what had happened to him. He found humor in what Lola said, and managed a stifled laugh.

"Do you really think those stupid alley cats are going to do what you tell them?"   "Let's find out." Lola raised her broom and shouted. "Charge!"

Using her broom like a Ninja stick-fighter, Mrs. B. struck Don rapidly with the handle. Focus anchored herself to his leg and used it for a scratching post. Duke climbed Don's back. Don stomped and spun trying to detach the cats. He managed to get around the furious broom swinger, out the door, and down the steps, all the time begging her to call the cats off as he headed for his limo.

As he ran, Focus continued to attack his leg and Duke had worked his way from Don's back to the top of his head. Lola followed, swinging the broom and shouting, "Yahoo, Ride-um-cowboy!"

Don cried in desperation. "Help! Call them off! Please! Lola saw he had had enough.

"Focus! Duke!" she called. "Let him go!" The two cats dropped off the wounded house burglar. Don reached the safety of his limo, slammed the door and held his handkerchief to his shredded scalp as he sped off. Seconds after the long black car left, Fred pulled up and dropped off Jack. The Ninja Housekeeper and two Ninja cats waited for him on the porch. Puffing from all the exertion, Mrs. B. felt good after her tussle. Both cats still had hackled hair.

Jack sensed something amiss. "What's going on? Has something happened?"

Mavis said to Audery, "Wasn't that exciting? I wonder what it all meant."

"What was exciting?" asked Audrey, as she tried to find her lost stitch.

Lola, Focus, and Duke, each tried to tell their version of what happened, but all at the same time, so all Jack could hear were three garbled voices talking about a burglar. He held his hands up.

"Whoa! Hold it! Slow down! What's this about a burglar?"

Lola, still excited and still holding her broom like a weapon said, "Let me tell it you two, then if I miss anything you can fill in the details. Okay?" Both cats mumbled that they could tell it better, but condescended to let her go first.

"While you were gone, a burglar broke into your house. He made a mess, but my gang and I. . .."

"Your gang! What gang?"

"Me, Focus and Duke, of course. We beat him up and ran him off! Focus saw him break in and ran to get me and Duke."

"Who's Duke?"

"Duke's my cat."

'You're my human is more like it.'

Jack headed for the door and they all followed him into the house.

"Did he get any of my cameras?"

"Duke doesn't think so. He frisked him before he got away." Jack checked to make sure and was greatly relieved when he found everything in its place and undisturbed.

"It doesn't look like he took anything, but with the mess he left, he was sure looking for something. Now, if I'm hearing this conversation correctly, am I to believe I'm in the presence of another talking cat?"

"It's true, all right. Somehow, he got into your hair muck and ate a small amount. It changed him as it did Focus; now we can all mind talk. I think these two are in love."

'You better believe it, sweetheart.' said the Duke.

"Lord, help us all," said Jack.

Meanwhile, Dr. Don Swaite, unsuccessful cat-burglar, was back in his lab in the Gray Pharmaceutical Building. He was extremely upset to say the least. Not only did he come away from his botched burglary empty-handed, but his body was bruised from a wicked woman's broom and his skin shredded by cat claws. After treating his wounds, he applied the last of several band aids.

"I'm not going to forget this soon. One day I'll have my revenge. That broom-wielding witch and those trained cats will rue the day they ever . . ."

His murderous plans were interrupted by the ringing phone. He grabbed it in anger.

"Hello! What! Who is this?"

"It's Fred! You grouchy jackass; I have another sample jar."

Don forced himself to calm down.

"Oh! That's great."

"When's a good time to bring it over."

"You can bring it over now. By the way, it's going to take a lot of this stuff to make a thorough analysis." He crossed his fingers. "How much of it do you have?"

While he talked Don doodled on a writing pad, his doodle was a large circle with a question mark in its center. Don held his breath waiting for Fred's answer.

"We have seven quart jars here and that's all their is. Will that be enough?"

Don's hand trembled as he scribbled the number seven over and over inside the circle where he had drawn the question mark. He tried to contain his excitement, but could not. He bounced in his chair and stomped his feet with glee.

"Don?" said Fred. "What's that noise?"

"I dropped a glass beaker. Sorry. Yes, seven jars should be enough. Bring me one jar as soon as you can and when I need more, I'll call you. But for now, meet me in thirty minutes in front of the Gray Building next to the news-stand. After he hung up, Don jumped to his feet and shouted.

"Fred! You don't know it, but you gonna save my ass!"

Fred was at the news stand on time and looked around for Don. Don limped from behind the stand; his bandages were bloody.

"What happened to you? Did you have a car wreck?"

"Not that simple; I got mugged by a vicious old lady."

"Really?"

"Don't worry about it. Do you have the jar?"

Fred had the jar under his arm wrapped in a plain brown paper bag. He held it out to Don who snatched it away from Fred, stuffed it inside his coat, and looked around furtively.

"Why are you acting so cautious?"

"I don't want anyone in the company to know what this stuff is or where it came from. Some of my colleagues might try to steal it."

"How long do you think the analysis will take?"

"A week; maybe more. I told you before; these things take time. You must understand, I have other things to do besides screw around with this project of yours, and, I might add, at no cost to you. When I have something solid I'll call you."

"There's one thing I'll say about you, Don, you're consistent; always the perfect horses-ass."

"Thank you Fred, I didn't know you cared--I have to go." Don turned abruptly, held tightly to the jar of hair muck under his coat and walked briskly through the side entrance of the Gray building.

Although Don never asked Fred directly where he put the remaining six jars of hair growth stuff, he was certain Fred and his friend had taken them to the college lab.

After a trip to the local market to collect a few things, he felt he had the upper hand in his game of deceit.

Late that night, Dr. Don Swaite sat for quite awhile in the limo watching the chemistry building at the college. He wore a ski mask and dark clothes to make sure he wouldn't be seen or recognized when he collected the jars. Patience was not one of his virtues, but living dangerously was, and he could wait no longer. On the seat beside him were two bags, each containing three jars similar to the ones he had already stolen. Their difference being, they held molasses instead of the muck.

Gathering the bags, he walked quickly to the lab building. His dark clothes blended with the night.

Luck was with him--he found the same window unlocked as before, opened it, and lowered the bags to the floor. The hard part was getting his chubby butt through the window; however, out of desperation, he managed.

Don was a logical thinker and took a calculated guess that the most likely place to look for the jars was in the refrigerator. He was right on target and switched the muck jars with the molasses jars. He then let himself out through the building's front door with the last bottles of the hair-growth concentrate. Now he had all eight jars.

Less than an hour had passed since Don's break-in. With the jars safely stashed out of sight, Don sat at his computer making entries.

"Okay--I know how much hair growth cream can be made from a pinhead sized portion. Five pinheads of muck make one drop, and I know how many drops make a quart." He punched in additional information and touched Enter on the keyboard. "Now then, machine, tell me how much hair growth cream can be made from eight quarts of concentrate."

The machine labored for five minutes without stopping, and when it did stop, Don had a hard time believing the numbers.

"That's astronomical!" he whispered, then he shouted. "Hot damn! Now I'll have all the time I need to find out what's in this stuff."

TWELVE

Don ran his calculations two more times before he accepted the numbers as fact. When he was sure of the production figures, he called Chairman Gray, as instructed. Within hours, Gray had started the publicity and production ball rolling. He then called a secret meeting in the board room. Present were his clones, the people from the production lab, the promotion and publicity staffs, and Dr. Don Swaite.

Chairman Gray entered the boardroom, locked the door behind him, walked to his place at the head of table and smacked a gavel on a wooden block several times until he had everyone's attention.

"Find a seat if you can. If you can't, stand. I don't care which." He gestured to Don. "Don, you come sit here next to me. First off, I want to be sure you can all hear my voice clearly--Well! Damn it! Can you? Let me see some hands." Every hand in the room shot up. "Good!" He took a long pull on his cigar. "Now then. There are a couple of reasons for this meeting. The first one is to congratulate Dr. Swaite on his development of Gray's Hair Growth Cream. The second reason, and just as important, is to sign a contract between the company and Dr. Swaite. Let's give Don a big hand."

Resounding applause, whistles, and shouts filled the room. The Chairman cut it short by banging the gavel again and shouting above the din.

"That's enough! That's enough. I wouldn't want all this attention to go to Don's head." Everyone laughed at Gray's attempt at humor, but behind it, Don knew the Chairman was serious.

"While I have your attention, there is one more thing I want to get across to you, and by damn you had all better listen closely to my words." There was a deathly silence in the room.

"The events taking place here and elsewhere within the company involving the cream are to be kept secret. In-house. No information will be released until I give the word." Gray paused, then continued, "Does everyone understand? Give me a show of hands!" Once again hands were above heads.

"In the event of an information leak, the person responsible will be found, and, most likely, that person will disappear without a trace." He was smiling when he said this. There was sporadic, nervous laughter from different groups. Those employees who had worked there any length of time knew it was a threat to consider real. The silence continued as Gray looked from face to face until he was satisfied they had taken his statement to heart.

"All right! Let's get this contract signed. You photo people. Pay attention, I want pictures of the signing and of Don and myself together. These pictures will be released later. Don, sit right here and use my pen."

Gray's clones crowded around trying to get close to Don, the new star of the company. Gray shoved one clone roughly aside and stood over Don, then he smiled for the flashing cameras as Don signed the contract. Cameras flashed again as Gray signed, then Don stood and shook hands with the chairman.

"That makes it binding, my boy. I wouldn't be surprised if this deal turned into a junior partnership." The clones, upon hearing this, went into a huddle in the background. They knew Gray never kept more than six partners at a time; that meant one of them had to go. Gray knew the clones would be in distress when he announced the partner possibility and he took great delight in their discomfort.

The chairman beamed a happy smile, then continued, "This hair growth cream should make millions for both of us, and that's only the beginning, my boy."

Gray slapped Don on the back hard enough to make him cough and to sit back down; this was the chairman's version of being friendly. During all this, the cameras continued to click. Gray picked the contract up and held it toward the cameras, and although the contract blocked Don's face, it was of little consequence to Gray. Don was oblivious to this anyhow. Totally overwhelmed, he stared hypnotically at the back of the contract and slipped into a dream state. Don saw himself surrounded and pampered by beautiful women aboard his yacht. Reality returned to him abruptly as Gray dismissed everyone in the room and told them to get back to work. This included Dr. Don Swaite.

*   *   *

Jill knocked on Jack's front door. Jack answered it and saw she was alone.

"Where's that asshole lawyer? Aren't you afraid to be here without him?"

"Please! Jack. Can I come in? I need to talk to you."

She seemed almost sincere, but Jack wasn't about to let his guard down.

"I guess so.   Yeah, come on in."   Jack suspected something devious was in the works, and before closing the door, he checked out front. By chance, through a thin place in the ivy, he caught a glimpse of a red car parked a half-a-block away.

He thought, 'That has to be Bert's car. I wonder what's going on.'

Jack followed Jill into the living room. She sat on the couch and hiked her dress high above her knees, as if she were posing herself for Jack to take her picture. Then she patted a spot next to her.

"Jack--please--come sit here, next to me."

Jack was really suspicious now.   Then Focus sent him a message from her spot on the back of the chair by the front window.

'Jack! There's a man sneaking around on the porch.'

Without looking at Focus, he sat next to Jill. Focus jumped to the window ledge between the curtains for a better look.

'It's a set-up, the man has a camera.'

Jack smiled at Jill, but projected a message to the watch-cat. 'Thanks Focus--keep an eye on him.' From the corner of his eye, Jack saw the man move swiftly past the window, camera in hand. Jack continued to smile at Jill, and wondered what she had to gain by this staged scene. Jack figured he had nothing to lose and would go along with her; just to see where this farce was headed.

"What did you want to talk about?"

She edged closer to him, put a hand on his leg and stroked his hair, as you might stroke a dog.

"I'm having . . ."

"Just a minute, stay where you are. I want to see you in full light." Jack left the couch, went to the window and pulled the curtains open wide, so the man with the camera would have a better view. The man on the porch saw Jack's approach to the window and Jack saw him scramble against the wall, trying to stay out of sight.

Jill thought, 'Jack, you're dumber than I realized. Opening the curtains will make this easier than Bert planned.'

'Jack, you're a crafty devil,' beamed Focus.

Smiling, he returned to the couch and sat close to Jill, put his arm around her and pulled her to him. For a second it seemed like old times, but his bitterness reminded him it was not.

"Now, what did you want to talk about?"

"I'm having misgivings about Bert. He's not the man I . . ."

Jack laughed a false laugh, "Well hardy-har, do you mean your lawyer, Bert, or your lover, Bert?" Her anger at the remark started to surface, but she fought it and ignored the remark as she continued with her memorized dialogue.

"What I really want is to get back together with you. I think your hair is very attractive. It turns me on. I would love to feel you next to me in bed." It was clear to Jack that Jill was forcing herself to sound seductive. Even her embraces and her kisses were forced as she stroked big dog Jack. Jack didn't care. He was enjoying himself.

At the window, Jack could tell the man with the camera was having trouble getting a clear view because Focus was in the way. Jack sent her another message,

"Focus, get out of the way so he can get a good shot."

'Sorry,' she said, and jumped to the back of a chair.

Jack supposed the man was getting pictures as evidence, or whatever they might be used for. In his mind, Jack imagined what they might look like if they were presented to a judge as evidence in her palimony suit and the reaction of the Judge when he saw them.

"Mr. Simon! This is your evidence? A picture of your client making love to a man in a monkey suit. I should have you disbarred! Now get out of my court!"

Jack laughed in the middle of an impassioned kiss.

"Why are you laughing? I assumed you wanted this too." She tried to look hurt.

"I laughed because I'm so happy you want me back," he lied. They went into another clinch and Jill tried to pull the hairy beast on top of her. He could hear the camera clicking away from outside the window. Jack broke the steamy clinch and pushed Jill away.

"What's wrong?" asked Jill.

"I almost forgot! I left the water running in the dark room. Don't move. I'll be right back."

Jack, followed by Focus, rushed from the room. When he was out of sight, Jill unbuttoned her blouse, hiked her dress as high as she dared, then gave the man at the window an okay sign. Meanwhile, in the darkroom, Jack bent over in front of the refrigerator door and ran his index fingers along the bottom edge, collecting a small amount of hair muck on each.

Focus watched. 'You're a sadist, and I think I know what you are up to. I love it.'

"I just can't help myself."

Jack returned to the living room and Jill. She had posed herself to look seductively inviting in a way that used to excite Jack. Jack sat next to her.

"Now, where did we leave off?"

"Right here, if memory serves me," She took Jack's face between her hands and kissed him. Jack took Jill's face between his hands and kissed her, then looked longingly into her eyes as he traced her upper lip, her eyebrows, and her chin with his muck-coated-fingertips.

The man at the window took more pictures.

Jack leaned back from Jill and looked as serious as he possible could under the circumstances, and said, "It will be great having you back, but there is one thing you must realize," he paused for effect, then continued, "I'm different. I'm not the same man I was. You would have to take me back for what I am."

"Oh, I will Jack. It will be a love story like Beauty and the Beast. Our love will . . .." She stopped and said suspiciously, "What do you mean, take you back for what you are?"

"It's not only my hair, it's--I can't explain exactly what comes over me--but the hair muck changed me inside as well--in my brain. Oh, I'm all right, most of the time, but on full-moon nights, I sort of black out and I'm not sure what happens. I never remember afterwards, but before these attacks start, I have these strange urges to take off all my clothes and howl," Jack looked at her intently, and breathed rapidly before he continued.

"Then I get a craving for raw meat and human blood."

Jill's eyes went wide with fear. Unsure of how to handle this unplanned twist, she slid away from him and buttoned her blouse as fast as possible. Jack shouted at her angrily.

"Why did you pull away from me?"

Jill shouted back at him. "Because you're scaring the pee out of me; that's why."

Jack jumped to his feet and started removing his clothes.

"Ohh! I can't stop! It's happening again! I can't . .." He threw his arms wide, his head back, and howled. "Ahooo! Ahooooo!"

He tore at his clothes until they were off, jumped onto the couch and growling menacingly, he said in a gravely voice, "I-want-you!" As he reached for her, she screamed, scrambled over the back of the couch and ran for the front door. Taking a quick glance back over her shoulder, she saw Jack crouched low and creeping sideways towards her, his arms swinging from side to side in front of his knees; just as an ape would move. He growled. She screamed, "Get away from me! You're crazy!"

She finally got the door open and flung it wide, then, as fast as her legs would carry her; she ran from the house. On the porch, she put on a burst of speed and sailed off the porch without touching the steps.

The man with the camera had seen enough of this strange scene. Clearing the porch rail with a running leap, he landed in a bush. Untangling himself, he escaped into the neighbor's yard.

Jill hit the ground running and didn't stop until she reached the safety of Bert's Porsche. Once inside, lover Bert laughed and pointed at her.

"What's so damned funny? I'm being chased by a homicidal mad-man and you think it's funny."

"Look in the mirror--you'll see why!"

She pulled the visor down and looked in the mirror. What she saw caused her to turn red with rage and to speak through clinched teeth, "I'll kill him. I'll kill him."

The comical image that looked back at her from the mirror had thick dark eyebrows, a fine mustache and goatee. She looked like one of the three musketeers.

Jill shouted, "He's a dead man! I'll kill him." Jack would have followed her except he couldn't. He was writhing on the floor with laughter. Still laughing, Bert started the car, made a U-turn and drove off while Jill pounded him with her fists.

Focus said, 'I wonder if that man with the camera got a picture of Jill sailing off the porch. That's the way I will always remember her.'

About that time Duke wandered in. 'I just saw Jill and Bert leaving in a big hurry.' Duke then saw Jack lying on the floor of the entry hall laughing. 'What's the matter with Jack?'

'I couldn't begin to explain.'

'These humans are strange. Are you sure it's healthy for you to hang around them?'

'I don't know if it's healthy or not, but it sure is fun.'

Jack finally composed himself and called Fred.

"I was wondering if you heard anything from your friend, Don?"

"No, I haven't. I've tried repeatedly to reach him at his office and at home, but he's never in. I guess he's just busy."

"I have a funny feeling about this, Fred, and I don't like it one bit. Be sure to call me the second you hear anything."

Duke and Focus sat on the back of the sofa looking out the window.

'I don't blame Jack for being concerned, I wouldn't be at all surprised to find out that Fred and his buddy Don were trying to steal Jack's stuff.'

'Maybe the Ninja cat should pay those guys a visit. What-da-yah think, sweetheart?'

'I think that's a very bad John Wayne impression.'

'That wasn't John Wayne! That was Bogart.'

'Whatever.'

THIRTEEN

That night Jack carried his microwaved dinner to a tray set up in front of the TV. He turned the boob-tube on to his favorite news station. Focus and Duke watched him from the back of the couch.

'Hey Jack, how about fixing something special for us?' said Focus.

'Yeah, my human friend,' said Duke. 'How about a half a tuna?' Jack just looked at him. Duke said, 'No tuna? Okay. I'll have what she's having.'

"It's times like this that I wish I couldn't hear you guys."

'He's a guy. I'm a gal,' Focus responded.

"Whatever," said Jack.

He finished eating by the end of the news, carried his empty tray to the kitchen, opened a couple of cans of fish catfood and put them on the floor. Jack fixed himself a dish of ice cream, poured on some chocolate topping, and took it back to the living room just as the movie of the week started. The announcer was in the middle of his opening spiel.

"Tonight! Our show is brought to you by your friends at Gray Pharmaceuticals Company. In a few minutes, GPC will introduce a new product that men and women all over the world have been waiting for. But first, sit back, relax, and enjoy the first act."

'It must be something very special,' said Focus.

"You didn't eat much," said Jack.

'I ate as much as I wanted.'

Duke joined her on the couch next to Jack. Jack finished his ice cream and when the next commercial break came on, he headed for the kitchen.

"I'm going to have a beer. Want one, Duke? Focus? You guys are great company."

'Smart ass!' said Duke.

'I'm a Gal. He's a guy,' said Focus.

Jack wasn't paying any particular attention to the commercial. While he put away his empty dish and the TV tray, Focus raced excitedly into the kitchen after him, 'Jack! I think you should come see this commercial.'

He returned to the room in time to hear the announcer say over a sequence of shots showing hair growing on heads: ". . . and this revolutionary new product, GHG cream, for growing hair was developed after years of secret research and development by Dr. Donald Swaite of the Gray Company. And listen to this introductory offer. GHG cream is available at your local pharmacy, but here's the astounding news. It comes with a money back guarantee. Stay tuned."

Dumbfounded, Jack turned pale, felt weak in the knees and had to sit. Slowly, his mind returned to the reality of what he had just heard.

"Did I imagine what I heard. I must have. Either that or I'm cracking up, that's what it is. It couldn't be right."

'I'm afraid you heard it right,' said Focus.

"It was Fred! That rotten bastard Fred sold me out!"

Jack jumped up, ran to the phone in the kitchen and

called him. It was difficult to sound calm.

"Fred! Hi, I have a question."

"What is it, Jack?"

"Would that old college buddy of yours happen to be the Dr. Donald Swaite that works for Gray Pharmaceutical?"

Fred was hesitant. There was silence for a minute before he answered, and caution in his voice.

"Yes--that's who he works for. Why do you ask? Is something wrong?"

It was difficult for Jack to continue talking calmly.

"I just heard his name mentioned in a commercial during a break in the movie. Why don't you turn on Channel 10 and see if they mention him again? Okay, Fred?" Jack didn't wait for him to answer, but hung up quietly and returned to the show. Then he exploded and shouted at the TV set.

"This - has - to - be - a - coincidence! Someone! Please! Tell me it's not true!"

Fred was confused by Jack's call.

"Why would Don be in a commercial, and why did Jack act so strange on the phone?" Fred did as Jack asked and switched the dial to Channel 10. The show was in the middle of a commercial break. Fred sat and listened, his heart sank when he heard.

" . . . So let GHG cream change your life. Never let baldness interfere with your happiness again. That's what Dr. Donald Swaite had in mind when he invented this astounding hair growth cream. Don't put it off another second . . ." Fred's mind stopped working and his hearing shut down, blocking out the rest of the commercial. In a trance, his face a blank, he stared at the television set. Reality fell on him like a cut tree.

Fred shook his head slowly as he repeatedly shouted the words, "NO! NO! NO! Don, how could . . ."

The phone rang somewhere in the distance. It rang several times before he reached for it. Traumatized, Fred answered, sounding as if he had been asleep.

"Hello?"

"Was that your old, trusted, pal from college?"

Fred was near collapse. "Yes, I'm afraid it was, but I . . ."

Jack could no longer hold back his anger and launched a vicious verbal attack.

"You dirty, rotten, back-stabbing, dirt-ball. I should have strangled you when I had you by the throat. You're nothing but a scuzzbag, egg sucking, chicken thief!"

Jack hung up as if he were driving nails. His anger was so intense he almost passed out, but he managed to stagger to the kitchen table, slump into a chair and bury his face in his hands. Focus and Duke, sensing his mental distress, jumped onto the table and put their paws on his arm trying to soothe his mental anguish.

Still in shock; Fred dialed Don's phone number.
"Gray Company, home of GHG cream, may I help you?"
That brought Fred out of his stupor.

"Yes! You can help me. Put Dr. Don Swaite on the phone. This is Fred Wong calling."

"Dr. Don Swaite's office, how can I help you, Mr. Wong?"

"I must speak with Don; it's urgent, so don't you dare put me on hold!"

"You don't have to shout, sir! Dr. Swaite told me all about you and how you tried to steal a lifetime of research from him, you wicked man. Dr. Swaite will not be taking any calls in the near future, especially from you."

With that she cut him off. Fred realized the futility of trying to reach Don again and hung up. He felt paralyzed and could not move from the chair. Anger, frustration, and confusion ruled his mind-then the questions began to come.

"How did they get the GHG Cream on the market so quickly. I have an idea--I think the answer is in my lab at the college--I'm going over there."

When Fred arrived at the Lab, the first thing he did was remove a jar from the cold box and hold it up to the light.

"This jar is not as heavy as I remember and it's a lot clearer than it should be." Unscrewing the lid, he smelled the contents.

"Molasses?"

One by one, Fred took off all the lids and discovered they all smelled the same. Hesitantly, he touched his finger tip to the liquid, smelled it again and apprehensively tasted it.

"It is molasses! That sneak thief Don broke in here and switched the jars." Fred grabbed the phone and called Jack.

"Come on Jack--answer the phone." It rang ten times, and when Jack didn't answer on the eleventh ring, Fred hung up, screwed the lid back on a jar, put it in a bag and left for Jack's house. On the way there, he repeatedly searched his mind, trying to determine how Don got away with the deception so easily. His only conclusion was, "I should never have trusted or put any faith into my former friend, Dr. Don Swaite."

By the time he reached Jack's street, his anger with his old college chum had built until he was mad enough to chew sand and like it.

Tires screeching, he turned into Jack's driveway,

bounced off the curb on the right side and slid to a stop halfway onto the front lawn. Grabbing the jar, he jumped from the car, dashed to Jack's front porch, and pounded on the door until Jack opened it.

When Jack saw who it was, he slammed the door before Fred could say a word. Fred pounded the door again and shouted at Jack.

"Damn it, Jack, open the door and talk to me!" He continued pounding until Jack jerked the door open again.

"How do you know I won't knock your head off!"

"Because I won't let you! You're going to listen to me, even if I have to knock you down and sit on you."

"What do you want, another shot at me? Haven't you done enough?"

"Wait a second. Let me show you something," Fred brought out the jar of molasses, unscrewed the lid and stuck it under Jack's nose. "It looks like the muck, right? Smell it. Take a good long snoot-full," Jack took the jar from Fred and smelled it again.

"Molasses? That's not hair muck, that's molasses!"

"Jack, I'm tired of shouting. You must believe me. Both of us have been had by Swaite. You might not think so at this moment, but I'm still your friend. Can I come in so we can talk about this?"

Jack just looked at Fred for a few seconds before he spoke.

"If you're telling me the truth, then I apologize, but if you're not, you won't get out of here in one piece. I guess I believe you, come on in old friend."

Fred followed Jack into the house. "Let's go into the kitchen and have a beer."

Jack fetched two brews and they sat at the table as they had often done in the past. Fred put the jar of molasses in the middle of the table.

"I'm as angry at Don as you are. I really believed we could trust him," Fred paused, reflecting on the situation, then he continued, "I never realized how naive I am. I'm sorry I ever met the conniving thief. I can't believe he's the same man I roomed with. In college, he was a full fledged jerk, but never dishonest."

"I understand your anger. Like you, I'm still so damn mad I'm shaking. What can we do about this situation? We certainly can't let him get away with stealing the Muck, and profiting from it too. How did you discover what he did?"

"After you called, I tried to get through to Don, but I couldn't get past his secretary. That's when I got the idea of what happened and went to the lab to confirm my suspicions. I hoped I was wrong, and at first it looked as if I were wrong, because the jars were all there, but when I opened them and discovered the molasses, I knew we had been tricked and I knew it was by Don."

"Molasses," Jack repeated. "So the thieving scum bucket has all the muck concentrate."

"All of it, every last drop."

"What does Don look like?"

"Short, over-weight, rotten attitude."

"That's the same description Lola Bobo gave of the guy that broke into the cat's house, I mean my house. That's when he got beat up and run off by my gang."

"Your gang?"

"You know, Mrs. B. and the two cats, Focus and Duke. Between her broom and the cat's claws; they must have shredded his hide."

"I wish I could have watched that action. I must have seen him just after he broke in here looking for the concentrate. When I saw him, he was limping and his head was covered with bloody bandages."

The next morning Fred and Jack lounged in the living room, still trying to figure out what to do. The phone rang; Lola answered it.

"City zoo--Jack! It's for you, it's your sweetheart."

He took the phone from Lola and said, "Ex-sweetheart. What does she want? Hello Jill. How's the bearded lady? Did you shave this morning."

"I'll get even with you for that if it's the last thing I ever do. I hate you!"

"Think positive. You can always get a job with the circus. Is that what you called about?"
No it's not. Those commercials I've been seeing onTV about GHG hair growth cream--is that your stuff?"

"I wish it was-but all the hair growth concentrate I had was stolen . . . "

"Sure, Jack, I'll just bet it was. I don't want to hear your lies. Anyway, the reason I called was to congratulate you on our big money deal with the Gray Company."

"Jill, listen to me, I . . . "

"I really hope it was for a lot of money so we can both be rich, especially me!"

"Jill! You must listen . . ."

"My lawyer will be around to collect my share! Good by."

Jack shouted into the dead phone. "There's nothing to share! You greedy woman!"

Mrs. B. said teasingly, "She was such a sweet thing."

"In her sleep, maybe."

Jack walked back into the living room and stopped in the doorway because Fred suddenly burst into laughter. He pointed at Jack and was unable to speak.

"What's so funny?" he said and looked confused.

'Duke,' said Focus, 'Look at Jack!'

'Well I'll be whipped,' said the Duke. Both cats jumped off the table and ran to Jack. Fred continued to laugh and point at Jack's feet. Struggling with hysterics, he finally got out what he was trying to say.

"Look! Jack. Look at your feet!"

Jack looked down and saw lose hair sliding out of his pant legs. He looked at Fred in surprise then looked down again. As he did, the hair on his head slid off and fell onto the cats who were having a ball playing with it.

The hair began to pile up on the floor. Jack shook his arms and more hair fell off. Taking his shoes off, he poured the hair from them as if it were water. Fred took hold of his Fu Manchu mustache and it came off. He tossed it onto Jack's pile of hair. Lola came in from the kitchen wiping her hands on a dish towel.

"What's going on in here?" She looked at Jack, then saw the pile of hair on the floor and the cats playing in it.

"Shedding, are we? Well don't expect me to clean up that mess."

FOURTEEN

Although Jack was extremely happy to be rid of his hair problem, there were others who were not. Take for instance a short over-weight man by the name of Dr. Don Swaite. His recent ill-gained wealth had given him a station in life he hadn't earned and didn't deserve. The new 'friends' he attracted were drawn to his money. Their false smiles masked true feelings of distaste for this new-money slob who feigned having culture.

His newly acquired, newly decorated, penthouse came with a maid, a housekeeper, and a cook. On an ill-fated evening, Dr. Swaite was entertaining an attractive young woman from New York, named Chelse.

Big band mood music played softly in the background. Before the main course arrived, the maid had served two steaming bowls of soup. Don raised his glass of white wine in salute to his guest.

"Here's to a wonderful evening, Chelse."

She responded in turn, "I'm looking forward to it, Don."

After sipping their wine, they put their long stemmed glasses back on the table. Don looked at her in a manner he considered suggestive. He thought, 'You will be my first trophy, Chelse. I have chosen you to help me celebrate my new digs and my new bed. Tonight's the night for you, my dear.'

Chelse smiled at Don and thought to herself, 'I know what you're thinking, you pudgy wart, but it's going to take a lot more than this puny show and a bottle of wine to get this girl between your sheets.'

Don didn't know which spoon to use for his soup, but to his way of thinking, he was rich and it didn't matter. He could slurp it from the bowl if he felt like it; however, he refrained from that urge and picked up a spoon. It was then he noticed a black hair in his soup. Naturally, he rang the silver bell and summoned the maid.

"There's a hair in my soup!" he said sharply, "Take this bowl away immediately and bring me another!"

"Sorry, sir," said the maid as she took the bowl and hurried off. As he looked at the blank spot formally occupied by the soup dish, he saw other black hairs. They stood out in stark contrast against the white table cloth. The maid returned with the fresh soup, and as she placed it before Don, an unnamed fear consumed him.

As casually as he could manage, he reached a trembling hand to his hair. The instant he touched it, a large clump fell off into his soup. With both hands he tried to hold his falling hair in place, but, like water through a sieve, loose hair slipped between his fingers.

Chelse watched his desperate attempt to stop the fallout, and began to laugh. Don however, cried out, "Oh! No!" Embarrassed, he turned scarlet red, then gradually his color changed to a shade of gray. He panicked, then shouted, "This can't happen to me! Chairman Gray will kill me!"

Chelse stood, picked up her glass of wine, walked around the table, and sloshed it into Don's face. The cold wine did keep him from going into shock, but did little for his ego. Chelse said, "That was, without a doubt, the most disgusting display of bad manners I've ever seen. *You're* the most disgusting thing I've ever seen, you bald-headed toad. Good night! Don't ever call me again."

With that, Chelse, from New York, let herself out and slammed the door behind her. Don, wine dripping from his chin, sat startled and staring at his bowl of hair soup.

"What the hell am I going to do?" He shouted to the room. Trying to think clearly was almost impossible. As he wiped the wine from his face, he shoved his chair away from the table, and began pacing the room. After a few seconds, an avenue of escape formed in his mind. He thought, 'One thing is for certain--I have to get the hell out of here and go into hiding.'

Don ran to the bed room, pulled out a travel bag, threw it on the bed and stuffed clothes and other things into it that he would need for a quick trip out of the country.

"I know what I'll do. I'll have plastic surgery. My friend, Dr. Hook will do it for me quick, no questions asked." Don looked in his directory, found the number and called.

"This is Dr. Hook. How can I help you?"

As Dr. Hook talked, he sounded friendly, but when he recognized Don's voice, a scowl distorted his face. The corners of his mouth turned down so far they almost touched under his chin. His distress centered on Don's voice and a pile of hair in front of him. "Yes, Dr. Swaite. Yes, I do remember you and how your commercials convinced me to use your hair growth cream."

"Never mind that," said Don. "I need to make an emergency appointment to have my face altered. Can you do that for me?"

"Why, of course I can," said Dr. Hook with a demonic smile. "If you like, I can see you right away."

"I don't want to look anything like I do now."

"I can definitely help you in that area, Dr. Swaite."

"You're sure I won't be recognized when you're through?"

"Dr. Swaite, when I'm through with you, no one will recognize you."

"Great!" shouted Don. "I'll be right over!"

Dr. Hook hung up and scooped his fallen hair into a waste basket, then directed a parting remark to Don.

"You jerk! When I'm finished with you, not even your mother will recognize you. I can hardly wait!"

*   *   *

In the apartment below Don's, two lovers slept back to back, their heads close together on the pillow. She had long lovely hair. His was dark and wavy. He turned to face her, but his hair stayed put on the pillow. She turned to face him, and her hair stayed put. The sudden feeling of airiness about their heads woke them. They looked at the pile of hair between them.

Startled, they sat up and stroked each other's bald heads. It was a turn-on for both. They fell back in bed and made love.

*   *   *

In the barber shop on the ground floor of the hotel, the barber asked his customer.

"How would you like it cut?"

"Leave the side burns. Cut the top short."

The barber ran a comb through the man's hair, and

211

it all came off. He handed the customer a mirror.

"How's that," he said.

*   *   *

In the conference room, Chairman Gray was presiding over a meeting with his clones. The clones all had their new hair combed in the same style as the chairman Gray. Gray was reading from the latest sales progress report and puffing on a cigar.

"I'm happy to report that sales of GHG Cream are twenty percent above our projected figure and climbing." Mumbled congratulations and polite applause were directed toward the chairman from the clones. As Gray studied the report, he scratched the top of his head. After soothing the itch, he couldn't help noticing the hair fluttering down past his eyes. His clones, of course, mimicked the chairman with the same results.

The chairman chomped down on his cigar. Frown lines cracked all over his face. "What's going on here?" said Gray in astonishment. He grabbed the phone and shouted, "Ms. Doxie! Get hold of that so called Dr. Swaite. I want to see him in the board room, and in front of me, pronto! Do you understand? Pronto!"

The rest of his hair fell off in a pile on the table. The clone's hair followed in unison. When the bulk of Gray's hair fell, it knocked his cigar ashes off and started a smoldering, smoking fire on the table. One fast thinking clone got a fire extinguisher and sprayed the smoldering hair. The force of the spray blew the hot hair into Gray's lap. Gray jumped to his feet and knocked his chair over.

While he attempted to brush the smoking hair from his pants, the clone brandishing the fire extinguisher, sprayed again and soaked Gray's lap. Not to be outdone, the other Clones jumped to their collective feet and knocked their chairs over. Gray grabbed the phone again and practically screamed, "Ms. Doxie!" She grimaced and held the phone away from her ear. "Get the security guard up here on the double and have him stand by your desk. When Swaite shows up, have the guard shoot him!"

*   *   *

Jack put the last dustpan full of rejected hair in a paper bag. Fred started to drop his Fu Manchu mustache into the bag, but changed his mind. "I think I'll keep it as a memento. I'll have it framed and hang it in the bathroom."

"I don't want to be reminded of the trouble this hair has caused. Mine is going into the trash."

"Well, Jack, that bag of hair brings to a close some events in our lives we won't soon forget. An end to a great fiasco, but remember this, the next time you have to blow off steam, stay away from the refrigerator. I'll see you later. Good-bye Mrs. Bobo," he shouted toward the kitchen.

"Bye, Fred," she said loudly.

Fred opened the door and left, but a few seconds later he came back in and stopped. His body blocked the view out through the open door. The silly grin on his face displayed delight over something only he could appreciate.

"What did you forget?" asked Jack.

"Nothing," he said, as he continued to grin, "There's a Charlie Fox here to see you."

Jack put the bag of hair down and leaned the broom against the wall.

"Who is Charlie Fox?" he said puzzled.

As he walked toward the door, Focus and Duke followed him. Lola looked around the doorway to the kitchen. As Fred stepped aside, he revealed an attractive woman standing on the porch. She smiled apprehensively.

Dressed for a field trip, she had a large camera bag slung over her shoulder and a travel bag sat at her feet.

"Are you Jack Stump?" she asked.

"Yes I am, but do I know . . ."

"I'm Charlie Fox--your camera assistant."

She held out her hand for a handshake. Jack took it and absently held onto it. She felt embarrassed. With everyone looking at her, she blushed.

"Could I have my hand back?" Flustered, Jack dropped her hand as if it were hot. He still felt puzzled about who she was, but as he continued to look at her a strange feeling crept over him--one he had never had before. Jack wondered, 'Is this love at first sight, or infatuation? I just met the woman, yet I feel a strong bond taking place, and I'm drawn to her rare beauty.' Jack felt joyful and short of breath in her presence.

Noticing Jack's stunned look, Charlie said, "Jack, are you all right?"

Jack's mind had gone blank. Flushed, he stammered, "I'm-uh-fine; I just don't understand why you're here. Camera assistant for what?"

"I can see no one called you. I'm from Autumn Life Magazine, and we have an assignment together. Have you forgotten?" She let him take her hand again.

"I'm sorry for being so dense. Please come in. I was expecting a man assistant--I mean, well, you know. With a name like Charlie Fox, I'm sure you run into this confusion all the time."

"Don't worry about it; it's the editor's little unfunny joke."

Jack let go of her hand long enough to pick up her bag. Now, he couldn't keep his eyes off her. Mrs. B. smiled a smile of approval. Fred, still grinning broadly, stood just outside the doorway on the porch. As Jack guided Charlie into the house, he closed the door in Fred's face without realizing it. Fred took the hint and went home.

As Charlie walked into the living room, she noticed Focus and Duke trotting along next to her, "I like cats," she said, as she sat on one end of the couch. Jack sat on the other, facing her. Mrs. B. looked on from the kitchen.

"Tell me all about yourself," said Jack. "I mean, you know, your photo background--uh--experience."

"There's not much to tell. I've worked in the photo department for the last two years where I gained a lot of hands-on experience, and they gave me this assignment with you."

As she talked, Charlie placed her camera bag on the coffee table. Duke jumped up next to it, rubbed his neck on a corner, and began sniffing it. He projected to Charlie, 'Smells like you have a cat?'

"I used to have a dog, but now I have a cat," said Charlie.

'You heard my mind talk, Charlie. Hey! Focus, she can hear me. Isn't that great? Her camera bag smells like a Siamese, same as you.'

"That's right, Duke" said Charlie.

Jack, still enchanted by Charlie, had not been paying attention to the conversation.

"What's right?" asked Jack.

"Siamese," said Charlie. "My cat is Siamese, too."

Focus got into the conversation as she leaped onto Charlie's lap.

'My name is Focus; that's Duke, he's mine. Jack is my human. I like you a lot, and I think it's obvious that Jack does too.'

"This is wonderful. I like you too, Focus and Duke."

"How did you know their names?" asked Jack.

"I was in mind contact with them and they told me their . . ."

"You don't have to explain; they talk to me too, when they want to. They talk to Mrs. Bobo all the time."

Lola said, "This one's for you, Jack." She said it more to herself, but Charlie heard her and sent a mind message only Lola could hear.

'Not so fast, Lola. He's nice, but only time will tell if there is any magic here,' Mrs. B. smiled at Charlie and went back into the kitchen.

"I arrived early and decided to come by to meet you and to find out if you were over your strep throat."

"What strep throat?"

"Editor Smith said you were ill when he stopped by."

"Oh! That. Yes, I was out of sorts. It was hairy there for a few days, but I'm fine now."

"I got the strangest image of you when you said hairy."

"I'll tell you about it someday."

"I also wondered if you had foreseen any problems with the assignment? I know we'll be working together for a month or so, and I can see our association will be a good one. Maybe we could go over some of the assignment problems. . ."

Mrs. Bobo had gone to the clothes tree by the front door and had begun putting on her many layers of clothes. When she finished with her rubber overshoes, she went to the living room entry and said quietly, "Focus. Duke. Come on, let's go to my house. See you later, Jack; you too, Charlie." Neither of them heard her.

Lola Bobolinsky and the two cats walked out the front door and on to the sidewalk. Jack must have turned the radio on; she could hear strains of the song, "Pussy Cat, Pussy Cat" sung by Tom Jones. The music faded as the threesome headed for Lola's house. Focus and Duke trotted behind Lola.

'Do you think both of us can live at Mrs. B's while Jack and Charlie are gone?' asked Duke.

'I'm sure we can, and we'll even let Mrs. B. live with us.'

"I heard that," said Lola.

'Just kidding, Mrs. B. Guess what Duke?'

'What?'

'I'm pregnant.'

"You're what!" exclaimed Mavis to Audrey on the porch across the street.

NOTES

The short-short stories: "Critter Up A Tree"--"Frogs Have Necks"--"About Chipmunks, Cats, and Brooms"--"Hearth Cricket", and "The Boy Who Loved Crabs", are fictionalized events from Jay Kemp's life.

"Secret Formula", an original short-story by Jay, was first adapted to a screen play by Jay Kemp and Vern Harden, then lengthened to a novella by Jay.

The poem: "Cuddling Two", was a response by Carol Kemp to Jay's poem: "Cuddling".

Jay Kemp and his wife Carol live with their cat, Cleo, in Payson Arizona. Both are accomplished fine artists. Their works can be seen in many galleries and private collections in the U.S., Canada, and Europe.

Look for the SciFi thriller trilogy;

The Adventures Of Lhone.

To order a copy of : CRITTERS FROM THE THIRD PLANET, please enclose check or money order for $9.99 plus $2.00 for shipping and handling. NO CASH OR C.O.D.'S Please.

Allow four to six weeks for delivery. Offer good in the U.S. only.

Send to: CRITTERS PRESS
704 E. Skyway Ct.
Payson, Arizona 85541
(520) 474-2798

Acknowledgments

Without the help and guidance of my family, many friends, and peers from the Payson Area Writers Society, PAWS, this book would never have happened. Special thanks to Hubert Herrmann. His expertise with a computer saved me from many tight spots.

JMK
Payson, Arizona
November 19, 1995